I0763538

WOLF KISSED

LUNA MARKED BOOK ONE

HEATHER RENEE

ISBN: 979-8732620917

Line Editing and Proofing: Jamie from Holmes Edits

Development Editing: ALD Editing

Cover: Covers by Juan

Character Art: @kalynne_art on Instagram

DEDICATION

For Jane Catherine,
Roman is yours.
I love your face.

PS: I forgot to tell you one thing… there's a chance you might have to fight to keep your claim. Oops!

CONTENTS

Mystics and Mayhem vii

1. Cait 1
2. Cait 13
3. Roman 25
4. Cait 33
5. Cait 43
6. Roman 53
7. Cait 59
8. Cait 69
9. Roman 81
10. Cait 91
11. Cait 101
12. Roman 111
13. Cait 119
14. Cait 129
15. Roman 139
16. Cait 147
17. Cait 159
18. Roman 171
19. Cait 181
20. Cait 191
21. Cait 201
22. Roman 213
23. Cait 221
24. Roman 233
25. Cait 245
26. Roman 259
27. Cait 267
28. Cait 275

29. Cait 287
30. Roman 295

Stay in Touch 297
Also by Heather Renee 299
About the Author 301

MYSTICS AND MAYHEM

If you're new to Mystics and Mayhem, welcome! This is a world I began with my Broken Court series and one I hope to write in for the next few years!

You don't have to read all of the series set within this world as they can all be read on their own without fear of spoilers, but I hope you'll check them out! So far, there are only two of them—my dark fae books and this one, wolf shifters—and you can expect witches, vampires, and more as time goes on!

If you've read the Broken Court series already, you just might see a familiar character in this first book and expect even more as Luna Marked continues! If you haven't checked out Broken Court, look for a sneak peek at the end of this book! Happy reading!

TRAINING FIELD
ROMAN'S CABIN
VAUGHN'S HOUSE
PACK HOUSE
EMBRY'S HOUSE
GARAGE
EAST TEXAS PACK

1

CAIT

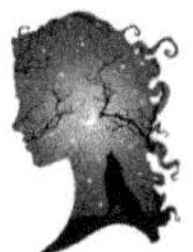

Boobs and abs. They were all I saw while wading in the waves on the Sydney beach. I'd been in Australia for a few months and admired their lack of give-a-damn. I hadn't jumped on the topless beach train, but those who did seemed to live carefree lives that had me slightly envious.

Taking the nanny gig here was something I had done on a whim in hopes of finding myself again after having spent the last couple of years traveling around the world without a plan. Well, other than to forget the pain I felt at losing a piece of me.

So far, Australia had been mostly screaming twins and showers three times a day, six days a week. The three-year-olds I cared for liked to throw their food at every meal. Their parents laughed while I grimaced at the evil beings disguised as toddlers.

It was nearing time for me to head back to the house. The water was warm, and the bright sun had been warming my exposed skin for several hours already, so I didn't have much to complain about other than my fingers and toes beginning to turn into prunes.

I pushed my arms through the surf, making my way back to the sandy shore. "Ouch." I yanked my hand out of the water, expecting to find blood with how badly my skin suddenly ached. Instead, all I saw was a red mark on my inner left wrist that looked like something had bitten me. "What the hell?" I muttered.

I kept my arms out of the ocean as I swiftly got back to the beach. I silently hoped the bite wasn't anything to worry about. It hadn't broken skin, and nothing was swelling. Yet.

The burning intensified as I got to my things on the sand. I searched for my phone, fully intending to Google what might have stung me, but was interrupted by warm droplets landing on my shoulder. A shadow cast over me, and I glanced up from my crouched position.

"Can I help you?" I asked, trying not to be rude in my haste to leave. Australians were some of the nicest people I'd met in all my travels.

His arm came up in a jerky motion as he ran his fingers through wet hair, getting even more water on me. I tried to focus on his face, but the sun was guarding it. Glancing down, I got an eye full of defined abs and black board shorts that hung just low enough to show off the muscled V leading south of his stomach.

"Who are you?" he demanded. His accent was American, taking me by surprise.

"I don't think that's any of your business," I retorted, matching his attitude and standing up to get a better look at him.

Holy hell, I should have stayed on the ground.

The man before me was tanned and muscled, but not bulging like he worked out three times a day in a gym. No, these well-rounded and defined muscles spoke of hard work. His shaggy brunet hair had golden highlights under the beating sun, and the scruff along his jaw added to the rugged vibe he was throwing off.

He barked out an angry laugh. "Who is your alpha?"

"The hell? Is that Aussie lingo for boss?" My brows furrowed, but he didn't respond. "Again, that's none of your business. Why don't you leave before I call the cops?" My iPhone was gripped in my hand, and I knew if I rapidly clicked the lock button five times, it would call emergency services. Well, at least, back home it would. Hopefully, it was an international feature.

I was trying not to overreact, but I wasn't dumb, either. Human trafficking was a real thing.

My heart was racing as he stepped closer, his breath brushing across my forehead as he looked down on me. I couldn't tell if my increased pulse was from fear or desire, because while I didn't want to end up as a prisoner, I wouldn't deny this man was attractive.

His dark blue eyes narrowed at me, and he sniffed the air around us. No, that couldn't have been right, could it?

He did it again, taking a big old whiff above my hair, not at all trying to hide his actions.

This was getting much too weird for me.

"I'm going to walk away now, and you're going to stay right here. Do you understand?" I used my serious voice that was normally reserved for the kids I cared for, all while trying to mask my underlying curiosity in him.

He shook his head, once again spraying water on me.

Before he could respond to my previous question, I couldn't help snapping at him again. "Will you quit acting like a dog and getting me wet?"

He smirked this time, some of his anger falling away as he lowered himself to my eye level. "I don't know what game you're playing, but I don't have time for witch games."

"You're insane, you know that? Seriously, though. I'm going to go." I bent down to grab my bag, my injury completely forgotten as I focused on keeping my hands to myself.

It didn't matter that my fingers had wanted to trail over his well-defined stomach muscles as soon as I'd laid eyes on them. The dude was out of his mind, and I needed to make a quick escape.

"No, you'll stay here until I know what you're up to," the guy said, voice deep and commanding. A tingling sensation settled over my skin that made my stomach tighten.

I hid the true emotions he was eliciting from me and

laughed while holding my bag and towel tightly in my grasp. "You, Mr. Stranger, don't get to tell me what to do. Take your brooding attitude and piss off."

He gaped at me, surprised when I took a step back. Apparently, he wasn't used to people disobeying him. Well, too damned bad. It was my only day off for the week, and I wasn't going to let the hot asshole ruin it. At least not all of it.

I turned around, and he grabbed my wrist to pull me back but let go quickly as the ache above my hand turned to fire. I winced, trying to fight back tears. "What is your problem, dude?"

His previously tanned face paled as he shook his head, staring at his palm. The guy was speechless, and I was done. Taking his shock as my chance to leave, I ran for the bus stop, sighing in relief as one was just coming down the street.

My feet moved rapidly, even though I couldn't stop myself from looking back at the stranger. He was still standing on the beach, face slack and body unmoving. I had to force myself toward the bus and not to turn around a second time to make sure he was okay.

I wasn't sure what was wrong with me. The guy had been a jerk, and whatever had happened when he touched me changed something—something that scared the hell out of me.

Remembering I needed my bus pass, I stopped trying to decipher what had transpired and dug into my bag. Just as the doors opened, I took one last peek at the beach, but the guy was gone. I sighed. Though, as long as he wasn't getting on the bus with me, it was probably a good thing.

I scanned my card and sat in the middle where I could see both doors. I shifted my eyes between the two until the driver closed them and pulled forward. No sexy stranger boarded after me.

The disappointment that rolled through me was ridiculous, and I distracted myself with my wrist. Lifting it up, I was confused to see the red was gone even though the pain had flared just moments before.

What used to look like a burn was now more like a birthmark just a few shades darker than my regular creamy skin color. The mark was a crescent shape with smooth lines, something a bite or sting wouldn't have been capable of, no matter the sea creature.

I took a picture of it and messaged it to my best friend Embry. She'd be sleeping on her side of the world in Texas, but after the day I'd had, I had a feeling that I would still be up by the time morning rolled around for her.

She'd been offline for a few hours, but as soon as my message went through, a green dot appeared next to her picture.

Me: It's after midnight and you have to work tomorrow. What are you doing awake?

Embry: What is that on your wrist?

Me: Dude, go to sleep. I'll tell you about it tomorrow.

I'd never met Embry in person, but she was my best friend. She'd joined a book group by accident, and I'd laughed at the comment when she admitted to not knowing why she was there, replying with a silly GIF. She immediately messaged me, and we'd been friends ever since. That was four years ago, right before my mom died of a heart attack at the young age of forty-six, and I graduated high school.

I didn't read as often as I used to. After losing my mom—my only parent—things changed in big ways for me, but I did my best to finish at least one book a month given it was something she loved so much. We used to enjoy reading at the same time and sharing opinions—mostly on the brutal cliffhangers we secretly loved but complained about.

Now, I didn't have that.

Without my mom, nothing was the same. She was my only family. The only person I'd counted on and my closest confidant. Until she wasn't. We'd lived a simple life, but it had been safe and secure. When she was taken from me so suddenly, I lost control of too much. I'd been fighting to get it back ever since.

After traveling for nearly three years, I still wasn't ready to go back to Oregon, but I'd also wanted a bit of permanency, too. When I took the job in Australia, I'd signed on for six months, but I wouldn't be renewing the contract even if they offered. I was ready to finish my travel list.

Six bus stops later, I exited onto the sidewalk and began walking to the house where I worked and lived. I only made it half a block before my phone started ringing.

"Embry? I told you we could chat tomorrow." I sighed, adjusting my bag as I held the phone to my ear.

"Oh, Cait. Shut your mouth and tell me what happened?" she demanded.

I laughed. "How am I supposed to tell you if I shut my mouth?"

She growled. "You know what I mean. Spill it."

"I don't honestly know. I was hanging out at the beach like I usually do on my day off. The water was warm, the air crisp. You know, just your usual perfect Australian day."

She sighed. "Yeah, I know. Australia is fabulous. You never want to leave. Blah, blah, blah. Get on with the good stuff."

I grinned. Messing with her was so fun. "Well, when I was getting out of the water, I felt like something had stung my hand. Given I'm in the land of deadly creatures, I kind of freaked out and rushed to get out of the water. Except when I looked at where it hurt, nothing was swollen or bleeding. Before I could think much more on it, this guy showed up. All muscled and wet."

"Muscled and wet? This doesn't sound like a problem, Cait. Did you lick him?" she asked, and I could hear the grin on her face.

"No, he was a jerk, and we never even touched." I didn't count his one-second wrist grab. "He got me all wet—"

She gasped. "He got you wet without touching you? That's talent. Can I meet him?"

"Damn it, Embry," I said, trying to sound serious, but ended up laughing instead. Now that I had her on the phone, the situation didn't seem as ominous. Well, except the mark on my wrist that was darker than it had been when I last checked on the bus.

I went on to tell her about the rest of the odd interaction. The more I told her, the quieter she got, which didn't bother me, considering it was the middle of the night for her.

"The picture didn't come in very clear, but you said it was like a quarter-circle?" she asked.

Looking at it again, I replied, "Yep, and darker now than before, but it doesn't hurt anymore. I'll get it checked out tomorrow. The family I work for has a pediatrician that comes to the house for the demon spawns, so maybe they can help."

"Umm, I'm going to ask you something that sounds really crazy, but I need you to know you can trust me. Okay?" She sounded nervous, and Embry was never anything but confident.

"Of course, I trust you, Em," I replied, pausing at the steps of the house.

"Do you know what an alpha is?" she asked.

"Like an alpha man? Sure, but I don't think that's what he was talking about."

She sighed. "No, Cait. Like alphas and betas and… packs."

"Packs? Like wolf packs? I don't think Australia has wolves around here. What would that have to do with the stranger?" She'd been right. She was sounding crazy.

"You really don't know?" she pressed.

"Know what?" I was starting to get frustrated.

Instead of answering, she requested a video call. I clicked accept and had my brow raised as her rose-gold hair, fair skin, and light blue eyes came into view. Her long strands fell in waves around her oval face, and her full lips were pinched.

"Show me the mark," she insisted.

I turned the camera from forward facing to outward, so I could see her reaction when she saw the burn.

Embry's eyes widened. "Shit."

I flipped the camera back to me. "You're starting to freak me out. What's going on?"

"Cait, I need you to trust me. You need to come back to the states. I can meet you in L.A. or you can fly into Dallas. Whichever will get you here sooner, but I need to see you."

"I can't just leave. I have a contract. I'll have to give them a full month's pay if I leave before the six months. I trust you, but it's not that easy," I said. I had cash saved from the odd jobs I'd taken during my travels, but it wasn't much, and I had to be careful how I spent it.

"Yes, it is." Her screen paused as she backed out of the video chat. I could hear her nails clicking on the screen before she popped back into view. "I just put the money in your account. I'm going to book you a flight and text you the details. Pay them, and get your ass to the airport. I mean it, Cait."

I was officially scared shitless. A text came through, confirming a new deposit had been made to my checking, and Embry was already off screen again, likely looking at flights.

"Am I in trouble, Em?" I asked.

She came back into view, her face softened. "I don't know. Just get here and I can explain better."

Embry was my best friend. It didn't matter that we hadn't met in person. She was scared, too, and as much as I should have asked a million questions before rushing back to the states, I did exactly as she asked.

I trusted her.

2

CAIT

The devastated look on the parents' faces when I told them I was leaving was enough to make me feel bad enough to consider staying—only almost, though. I packed as quickly as I could, so they couldn't guilt me into staying.

As I got in the car Embry had ordered for me, I checked my email. There was a first-class ticket for a direct flight from Sydney to Dallas, along with instructions to meet another driver who would be picking me up and taking me the nearly two hours to Embry's house.

First-class seats? Drivers? I was starting to believe Embry didn't do online marketing for a small company like she'd told me these last few years.

Her texts were few and far between as I gathered my belongings. Even when she did respond, it wasn't to answer any of the fifty questions I'd asked. I was beginning to wonder if I was making a mistake just taking off on a whim at her demands.

The driver chatted my ear off about the weather and tried asking me about the places I'd visited while in the country. Even with my minimal answers, he managed to keep the conversation going until he stopped at the terminal.

I waved goodbye once I had my bags in hand and took a deep breath. I could do this. Embry was my best friend. All I had to do was trust her.

Except, that faith wavered every time I caught sight of the mark on my inner wrist.

The color hadn't changed since I got back to the house, but I still marveled at how perfectly shaped it was. I hadn't had time to search for any answers online, considering I went from quitting my job to packing within the span of only thirty minutes.

Check-in was almost closed. I was cutting it close with the flight Embry chose, but since I was first-class, I cruised right through the bag drop and was even upgraded through security and customs. Luck seemed to be on my side.

My name was called over the speaker when I was still a dozen gates away from mine, and I was nearly panting by the time I shoved my phone into the flight attendant's face.

"I'm here," I heaved.

"Ahh, yes, Ms. Jones. We've been paging you. You're just in time," the lady scanned my electronic boarding pass and pointed to the hallway. "Just follow that down and someone will get you seated if you need help."

I nodded and waved my thanks while she closed and locked the door behind me. A young man was tapping his foot, likely waiting on my arrival.

Mumbling my apologies, I rushed to my seat, which was only four rows in and ginormous. As soon as I tucked my purse below, a flight attendant creeped in from behind.

"Good Evening, Ms. Jones. Can I get you anything to eat or drink before we take off?" she asked, smiling politely and not at all making me feel horrible for nearly causing a delay in take-off.

"Water and…" Crap. What did people eat in first-class? I was only used to the hard cookies or peanuts that were normally tossed out to economy seats.

She patted my shoulder. "No worries, dear. I'll get you a bottled water, and there's a menu next to you when you're hungry. A pillow and blanket are under your seat as well. Just press this button here if you need anything at all once we're in the air." She pointed to the panel above my head, and I glanced at her name tag.

"Thank you, Judith. You've been very helpful."

She nodded and ventured off while I figured out the seat controls. The seventeen-hour flight was going to be the best ever, I thought as I lay the seat back and rested my eyes.

The day's events had caught up to me, and I was asleep before she even came back with my water.

As soon as we landed, a heat settled into my body, and I found it difficult to breathe. Cool air was hard to find inside the plane, and it was even stuffier inside the airport with all the people milling about.

It was just after eight in the morning when I turned my phone back on. There were two texts from Embry: one telling me the previous driver had canceled and she was picking me up. The other said she'd had something come up and someone else was being sent. I typed a message back, wondering how the hell I was supposed to know who I was looking for, but she didn't respond before I had to go through customs.

After that chaos, I'd forgotten about Embry and was tempted to just take a taxi, except I didn't know where I was going. My head was pounding, my vision was blurred, and I was hangry. I thought I'd gotten enough sleep and food on the plane, but jetlag wasn't playing nice as I lugged my two suitcases behind me.

As I exited the doors of the Dallas airport, an August summer heat seeped into my bones. It felt like it was nearing one-hundred degrees and humid as hell. Why would anyone willingly live here?

I glanced around for the taxi line, but before I could find it, I saw a bearded giant holding a white sign with my name on it. He winked and waved me over to the sleek black sedan I didn't recognize the make of, but the chrome trim and sleek lines told me it was expensive.

His reddish-brown hair was shaved at the sides,

but long on the top and slicked back. His beard was the same color and several inches long. His light blue eyes sparkled with mischief as he continued to wave at me.

"Cait Jones?" he asked, and I nodded. "Fantastic. Give me your bag." His words were demanding, as if he was used to people doing whatever he said, but there was a kindness in his deep tone I hadn't missed, either.

"And you'd be?" I asked in return.

"Oh, right. We didn't talk about that."

I smirked. "No, *we* didn't. I don't make a habit of getting into cars with strangers."

He grinned back. "But you fly across the world to a place you've never been to stay with a girl you've never met. Good to know where your boundaries are."

His leather jacket flexed as he grabbed my bags and tossed them not-so-carefully into the trunk, then opened the back door for me. Good thing all of my important belongings were in storage back in Oregon.

"I'm Vaughn." His eyes leveled on mine, and I immediately wanted to look down.

The hell?

It took every effort I had to hold his stare. "Nice to meet you, Vaughn," I said through gritted teeth.

His gaze softened. "Interesting."

"What?" I asked.

"It's interesting to meet you." Vaughn's hands landed on my shoulders as he nudged me toward the seat. As I turned back to comment about him keeping his hands to himself, I caught a glimpse of another man in my peripherals.

How I'd picked him out in the crowds around us, I didn't know, but Vaughn stepped in front of me as I tried to get another look. "Something wrong, Cait?"

The way Vaughn said my name told me he knew things I didn't, and I wasn't a fan. I shoved at his chest, but by the time he was out of my way, the stranger from Australia was nowhere to be seen. Maybe it hadn't been him at all. More likely, I was just seeing things and having more jetlag side effects.

Glancing down, the mark still hadn't changed physically, but the throbbing within seemed to ebb and flow as time passed.

"Let's go," I huffed and slid into the back seat of my own accord.

He lowered himself to my level, eyes bright with excitement. "This is going to be so much fun." Then, he shut the door.

I pulled out my phone. There was still no response from Embry about how I was supposed to know who was picking me up, and I hoped like hell I wasn't about to become a statistic. The last few years had made me equally more trusting of people as well as more suspicious of them. I'd learned a lot on my own and grown up a lot faster than most twenty-one-year-olds. Loss had a way of doing that to people.

Vaughn turned on music, humming as he maneuvered the car like a professional driver through the cluster of vehicles in front of the terminals.

"Aren't you hot?" I asked as I took in the black leather jacket that hugged his broad shoulders to perfection and tight-yet-worn jeans that covered his long legs.

He coughed. "I mean, *I* know I'm good looking, but most women don't point it out so bluntly. Thank you."

I sighed. Heavily. "I meant your body temperature, biker dude."

"I acclimate well. Did Em tell you about Susy?" he asked.

"Who's Susy?"

Vaughn shook his head. "The beauty I should be driving. My one true love." He then proceeded to go on a tangent about his Harley motorcycle that I had zero desire to know about. The only positive was he'd mentioned Embry, or at least I assumed that was who he meant by Em since I often called her that, too.

I continued to text her as he rambled, but she never responded. I was going to kill her for doing this to me. The only positive was that Vaughn had put my mind at ease, and the pressure that had been building within my head was gone.

"So, what about you?" Vaughn asked.

"Uhhh, sure?" I replied, feeling guilty for not really listening to him. I was pretty sure he'd been asking about the ocean.

"Well, that might be a problem." His eyes met mine in the mirror.

Shit. What had I just replied to? "Sorry, I wasn't actually listening. To be honest, I'm a little worried about the fact that Embry isn't responding and I'm in the car with a complete stranger having no clue where I'm headed."

He nodded and smiled. "If you'd been paying attention, I wouldn't be such a stranger. As for where you're headed, it's one of the safest places in the world. You have nothing to fear from our pack."

"Our pack? Do you live with Embry? I thought she lived alone on her family's property." Things were getting weirder by the second.

"I think I'll let her explain. As for me, I think I like you, so I'm going to give you a second chance. Are you ready to listen?"

Now I felt like an asshole. "Yes. Please tell me all the things about you, Vaughn."

"My name is Vaughn Pierce, I'm thirty-five. I'm in a seriously committed relationship with Susy."

I butted in. "Isn't that your motorcycle?"

"She's so much more than that. You'll see once I get you on the back of her. Well, maybe. Anyway, I live for the land. A place where it's quiet and I can run with my… uhhh… myself. I also enjoy driving, which is why Embry sent me instead of anyone else. I'm very good at what I do."

Vaughn didn't look as old as he said he was, but he had an air of superiority about him that made me believe he was telling the truth.

"Thank you for the brief look into your life," I said as I stared out the window, trying to figure out what direction we were headed.

"Your turn," he said.

"I think I'll pass."

He made a grumbling sound. "Well, that's rude."

I'd offended him, and another wave of heat overcame me. Damn it, what was going on with me?

Vaughn continued to glower at me—even more so than the road he should have been watching—until I finally caved. "Okay, fine. I'm Cait Jones. Just Cait, not Caitlyn. I'm twenty-one, and I've never been in a serious relationship, not even with inanimate objects." Vaughn grunted at that but let me continue. "I enjoy the beach and traveling, and I'm not a fan of physical exercise, so don't expect to find me ruining your quiet place while you run."

"Where did you come from? How did you meet Embry? She just mentioned she'd never seen you in person," he said, finally focusing more on driving.

"A small town named Hope, Oregon, and a book group online."

He laughed, deep and loud. "Just another reminder about how not normal it was that you were hesitant to get in a car with a stranger, but you let someone you met online fly you to a place you've never been. Twisted, girl. Very twisted."

He had only the tiniest of points. Except Embry wasn't a stranger. We'd video chatted almost daily since our first year of friendship, and I was pretty sure I knew everything about her. Though, that confidence was fading by the hour as my anxiety ramped up.

After I'd zoned out for who knew how long—thank

you, jetlag—the car began to slow. I glanced at my phone, surprised it was just after eleven. Somehow two hours with Vaughn had already passed, yet still no response from Embry.

"Where are we?" I asked.

"Southeast of Dallas. Away from people."

The land was a rich green and clearly well cared for. Mature trees lined the paved driveway that had smaller dirt roads off of it. Another two minutes passed before a large structure came into view. It wasn't a mansion, but it was bigger than any house I'd ever been to.

The two-story home was light grey in color with white trim and a full wraparound porch that held a bench swing and a half-dozen chairs. While it looked well taken care of, something told me the house was like decades old, maybe even closer to a century.

On each side of the house were twin towers. Or, were they turrets? It wasn't a castle, so I was going with towers. Double red doors with massive frosted-glass windows opened as we came to a full stop.

"Welcome to our home," Vaughn said as he appeared at my door and I stepped out.

Before I could question him, Embry tackled me against the car. "I can't believe you're here!"

As mad as I was at her for her crap communication, I hugged her back just as fiercely. Tears fought to fall from my eyes as she rocked us back and forth. I hadn't known how emotional this moment would be. Seeing her on video was one thing, but feeling her tight embrace affected me like nothing before.

Over her shoulder, an older couple came out of the house. The woman had short blonde hair and wore a large, welcoming smile, but the man paid no attention to me as he looked beyond the car.

Curiosity got the better of me, and I turned as well. Another vehicle was coming up the drive, much faster than we'd been. The brakes protested as they were slammed, and the driver's door swung open.

Angry cobalt eyes stared me down. "What. Is. She. Doing. Here?"

Embry winced and stood in front of me as the older gentleman went to the guy that I'd seen less than twenty-four hours ago on an Australian beach. They looked a lot alike and I briefly wondered if they were related.

"Roman, come inside," the man said sternly.

"But she's a—"

"I said, come inside." The older man was nearly as upset as the guy from the beach, and I was back to freaking the hell out.

"Embry, what have you dragged me into?" I hissed, and Roman's gaze snapped back at me.

Heat consumed my body, and I stumbled against the car. Embry grabbed my hand, but I jerked it away as my wrist was consumed in agony.

Embry's worried blue eyes landed on my mark. "Come on. I'll tell you more as soon as we get to my place."

She had better tell me everything, not just *more.*

3

ROMAN

Normally, I prided myself on being a calm alpha, but every man had his breaking point and I'd found mine. All I'd wanted to do was take some time for myself. I'd arranged plans, involved people I didn't like, all for the sake of privacy. Yet, every time I turned around, the complete opposite was what I got.

I thought the best option was a secluded fae island where I could be in wolf form without worrying about being disturbed. Except those plans had been waylaid by the local fae. I'd recognized Lucinda as soon as I saw her and left the area right after she and her friends disappeared. If she was there, I knew not to be. From what the packs in Southern California said, Lucinda was nothing other than trouble.

Then, I tried for the next best thing. A human island. Something about the ocean and its waves always calmed my human half, but this time, I'd been stopped in my tracks.

My wolf had awoken and howled inside my head after sensing our mate was nearby. Finding another shifter in a populated place like Sydney had seemed impossible. Even more so when I found the woman my inner being claimed. She was either a witch, a human infected with witch magic, or something close to it.

At first, I thought she was a shifter, but then I caught her scent. There was nothing animalistic about it. She smelled of intoxicating flowers that should have been overwhelming to my wolf but, instead, had him humming with need right alongside me. Layered beneath the floral aromas were traces of citrus and mint.

I knew I needed the time away—I always did this time of year—but after the interaction, I had to get home. Someone was trying to mess with me, and I needed to make sure it wasn't an attempt to overtake my pack.

The day continued to get worse when I'd been stuck in economy seating and could still smell the female even though she was nowhere near me. I hadn't slept in nearly two days, and all I'd wanted to do when I got home was make sure my pack was okay and then disappear to my cabin.

Except that wasn't what happened. No, I arrived to find *her* there. On my pack lands. Fury like I'd never known exploded within me. At least that was the emotion I grasped on to when my eyes landed on her.

My father had sensed the rage first and urged me inside, but I couldn't move. When I'd tried to argue that the woman standing in our driveaway had to be some sort of witch, my father had spoken through our mental connection, reminding me I was the alpha. That I needed to remain calm and walk away before I did something that wouldn't fare well for the pack. He was right, and it would be smart of me to trust his judgement. I'd been letting my emotions guide my actions since seeing the woman. That needed to end.

I followed him inside as the woman disappeared with Embry, a pack member I was going to be having words with as soon as I spoke with my parents.

The unknown woman had been truly frightened by my outburst, and I couldn't deny that piqued my curiosity about her. The heat radiating from her scorched my skin as I'd glared at her, and nervousness poured from her in waves. Whoever had picked this woman to mess with me had chosen wrong.

Going through the double doors of the house, I followed my parents down the hallway and to the stairs leading to my office. Every step up the wooden stairs was precisely taken as I took control of my thoughts, preparing to figure out what the hell had been happening. Once the three of us were within the confines of my office, I closed the door with more force than I'd intended.

"Roman, I need you to listen," Dad begun, and Mom cut him off.

"The two of you are too much alike. Let me, dear." Mom smiled sweetly at Dad, but the two of us knew better. Mom was a control freak. If she wanted to lead the conversation, it was safest to let her do just that.

Dad waved his hand out and took a step back as Mom leaned over my desk, hands curling around the wooden edge and her gaze leveling on me. "Son."

"Mother."

"Embry came to us with suspicions about Cait. We've been trying to reach you. Before you go on a tangent, how about you tell us what happened? *Calmly*."

So that was her name. Cait. My wolf rumbled. He liked it.

I took a few deep breaths and dropped into my desk chair. Once I did that, my parents both sat as well. I explained what happened on the fae island and then in Australia while leaving the part out about my wolf calling Cait "mate".

"By the time I'd made it to the airplane, my phone was dead. I didn't have time to grab a new charger after accidentally leaving mine in my checked bag. What did Embry have to say?" I asked.

They shared a look I didn't like, and it was Dad who spoke next. "What do you remember about the Moon Goddess?"

"Seriously?" I deadpanned.

"Yes, Son. Seriously."

"She's our creator, born from the magic of the moon. Her first child was the first wolf shifter, bound to his wolf form during every new moon until he gained control over the beast within. Which was the only rule the goddess had in regard to the gift she passed along to her children."

My mother nodded. "Correct. What about her chosen children? The ones not directly descended from her?"

"The Marked? Not much. Why?" I asked. It was never a big focus in our learnings growing up.

"Our history books tell of a being called the Luna Marked. A child of the Moon Goddess who is neither wolf nor human, but is bound to the pack life," Dad answered.

They had to be shitting me. "Are you trying to say that this woman is Luna Marked?"

"We are. She showed Embry the mark, and you know Embry's memory. She recognized it right away. She didn't know that you were the wolf Cait had a run-in with, and she'd ordered Cait here straight away," Mom said.

"Why?" I managed the singular word through my rising anger, hoping they understood what I wanted to know.

"Apparently, Embry and Cait have been online friends for a few years now. Embry has always thought fondly of the human girl and enjoyed their chats," Mom answered again.

"Son, why does Cait's presence bother you so much?" Dad asked.

I shook my head. I couldn't say the words. I didn't believe what they were saying. None of this was right. I was the pack alpha. I needed a strong alpha female at my side. Not some watered-down version that had no clue about our lifestyle. The other females would tear her to bits.

"What happened with her?" Mom asked when I didn't answer Dad.

Tell them, my wolf finally chimed in. He'd been a quiet bastard since Cait walked away from us. I'd asked him a million questions and received little in reply. All he wanted was to get home.

Did you know she was coming here? I asked my wolf.

No, but I hoped, and you should be more grateful we don't have to search for her any longer.

Damn him. He likely knew about the Luna Marked stuff as well and withheld it on purpose. Wolf spirits were granted to shifters when they were born. Mine had lived two lives before joining me and had never found his mate. Fate was a bitch sometimes.

"My wolf thinks Cait is our mate, but he's wrong, right?" I asked them both.

As their heads turned toward one another, I slammed both of my fists down on the desk. "She can't be mine."

My voice broke at the end. My life had been hell the last couple of years. First with Dad's injuries, then the death challenge, and the pressure from the elders to choose any alpha female if I couldn't find my true mate. I couldn't bring this woman to them. She was not my equal, and it wasn't fair to her. There were expectations of me that someone like her wouldn't handle well.

"Son, I know you see only problems here, but I encourage you to read up on the Luna Marked. I sense your fear, and I believe it's misplaced. From what Embry has told us, Cait is a strong girl. I know this isn't ideal, but I also know finding your true mate is a blessing," Dad said, his words not at all calming me.

Your father is right, and you know it. You're just scared, my wolf added.

Not for the reasons you think.

"She knows nothing about wolves or the pack life," I said calmly, trying to remove my emotions from the conversation.

"She can learn. I'll teach her myself if needed," Mom replied.

No, we will teach our mate. It's our job, my wolf demanded, but I ignored him.

"Outside of our new arrival, the pack is safe?" I asked, and they each nodded. "I need time. I don't know how much, but don't expect me back for dinner."

I stood from my chair and they did the same. I hugged my parents tight. While the situation was the biggest shock of my life and I still had plenty more questions, I needed to shift. I needed to run. I needed to howl at the moon. Most importantly, I needed to do all of that alone.

"She'll be safe with Embry for now," Mom said as I pulled away.

My chest constricted. Did I care if the woman was safe? I did, and I couldn't deny it. At least, not to myself. Even though I'd denied the fact she could really be my mate and believed the work of a witch was at play, my wolf was powerful enough that I couldn't ignore his thoughts and feelings.

He saw things in black and white. There wasn't an in-between for him. He knew she was ours, and when I allowed myself to see it that way, I knew what I had to do—even if I didn't like it.

Once I had some time to clear my thoughts, I'd have to accept the curveball thrown at me. I'd have to find a way to make things work. Never mind that Cait didn't have a wolf. If she was really mine, the woman would be cherished and protected for all of her days.

But how many days would we get with her? Wolves lived long lives. A human couldn't live five hundred years, not even one hundred for most of them.

She's not human, my wolf reminded me, but it didn't mean anything.

I was ready to shift and disappear for a while.

Maybe when I got back, all of this would make a little more sense.

Wishful thinking on my part, I was sure.

4

CAIT

Embry led me down one of the dirt trails I'd seen on the drive in. She refused to answer any of my questions until we were at her place, and I was about ready to throw a rock at the back of her head.

Roman. That was the name I'd heard the older man call the guy from Australia, but giving him a name didn't make the situation any less weird. Something was happening, and whatever it was, it affected me. My mind was reeling with possibilities, but all of them were too wild to be true. Years of reading had done that to me.

We arrived at a small navy-blue A-frame house with large windows and a single wooden door. There was a sign above the entry that said, "Knock before noon and see what happens." I snorted at the words because they were very much Embry.

Inside was an open floorplan. I could see a bedroom down the short hallway, a bathroom next to that, and to my left was a modernized kitchen I'd seen glimpses of before. Though, our video chats hadn't shown how clean everything was.

There was a small pub table with three stools and a massive desk with three computer screens. "So, you really do have a marketing job?" I asked with a nod toward the home office setup.

"Um, more like watching the financial market," she replied while heading into the living room.

A massive fireplace was the center focus of the home. In front of the hearth was a coffee-colored sectional couch that curved so every spot had a view of the stone mantle.

"Have a seat. I'll get us snacks, then we can talk," she said and darted off before I could object.

I wasn't even close to hungry. I was tired and confused and so many other things I didn't understand.

Embry leaped over the couch, holding a tray of cheese, crackers, a bottle of wine, and two glasses. She landed on the couch gracefully and set the tray on the coffee table as if her movements were completely normal.

"So, you probably have a lot of questions," she began.

"Probably? Pretty sure I've asked dozens and you've answered all of… none."

She rolled her eyes. "No reason to get an attitude, Cait. I'm on your team."

"And what exactly does that mean? Who is Roman?

What am I doing here? And what is *here*?" I asked the questions in rapid succession.

"Ahh, the easy stuff. I'm glad we're starting there. Let's see, being on your team means no matter what Roman says, I have your back. You're my guest, and I won't let him kick you out. Roman is an alpha—like my boss. You're here because something happened to you, and I didn't know who you'd been interacting with. Not all of our kind are friendly, and I needed to know you were safe. Lastly, here is my home. Where I was born and where I will die. This is my pack."

None of those things made me feel any better. My palms were sweaty, and my knee bounced until Embry placed her hand over it.

"I know it's a lot and you have plenty more questions inside that head of yours that I intend to answer. I never wanted you to get wrapped up in my world. It's not anything like yours—or what yours used to be—but I promise you, whatever is happening, I will protect you with my life. You're my best friend, Cait," Embry added.

Holy hell. I couldn't breathe.

"What does *that* mean? How can your 'world' be any different than mine?" I asked in a panicked voice using air quotations.

"There's really no easy way to say it, but I know you can handle it. A small part of me has always wished for this day, but I hate that I have to do it like this."

"You're rambling, Em. Get to the point before I lose my shit," I said.

"I'm a wolf shifter. This is my pack. Roman is our alpha. Everyone who lives here are wolf shifters, and I think that maybe you're descended from one." She spit the words out so fast, I was certain I didn't hear her right.

I laughed. The sound started soft, then grew in volume as her face turned from worried to downright frightened.

Embry reached for my hand. "Are you okay?"

"Am *I* okay? I should be asking you that. You think you're a werewolf!"

She shook her head. "No, not a werewolf. A wolf shifter. Werewolves are what humans used to call us when we were first created by the Moon Goddess, but we have more control over our wolves now."

There was no humor in her gaze as she held on to me, her blue eyes begging me to believe her.

Embry's fingers traced over the mark on my wrist. "This makes you one of us, but I don't quite know how. I've spent the last sixteen hours since speaking with you trying to figure it out."

"You're fucking kidding me, right? This is all some joke. None of it can be real," I muttered as my energy began to wane.

"Yes, this is all very real. Would you like me to shift to prove it?" she asked with a wicked grin.

"Not a chance in hell."

"My wolf likes you. We had a bet on whether you'd cry or run screaming. Neither of us expected you to laugh," Embry said.

She had a bet…with a wolf? This was not getting any easier to wrap my head around. I glanced down at the mark and rubbed my thumb over it. The pulsing I'd grown used to already was dull at the moment, but the mark was warmer than the rest of my skin.

Roman had asked me who my alpha was, but then he'd also said something about witch games. Holy shit. *Witches?*

"Are…witches real, too?" I asked, and Embry nodded.

I then wondered how many things I'd always somewhat-jokingly wished were real actually were. If wolf shifters and witches existed, then… No. Not everything could be. It didn't make sense how that kind of thing could stay hidden from humans.

I felt like an idiot for asking but couldn't help myself. "What about vampires and fae and everything else?"

She grinned. "I'm not sure what 'everything else' is, but most likely. There is more supernatural in this world than most imaginations can make up, but we're not talking about that today. We're talking about wolves. Do you have a voice inside your head?"

"Not that I'm aware of. Am I supposed to?" I hoped not.

"I don't know. My mind is really good at remembering images, but words, not so much. It's why I don't like to read. I've seen that mark before, but none of us can find the history book in the pack library that speaks of it. Roman's parents, Jack and Ramona, knew some about it, but not enough that I can really give you any answers."

"Why is Roman so angry with me?" I asked.

She poured us both a glass of wine. "Roman has been through a lot. He's only been our alpha for two years, and his time leading hasn't been easy. He's one of the younger alphas at only twenty-six, but he's always been someone the pack admired, even as a child. I doubt he's angry *at* you. He's likely just upset about the situation. He likes to be in control. Given we don't know anything about you, there is little to control."

Embry sat next to me, just the same as I'd always known her: lively, happy, and gorgeous. It was hard to believe the words she was saying. Given I wasn't running out of the house screaming like she expected, I took that to mean shock had settled in, protecting my mind, and I'd be fine for the time being.

During my travels, I thought I'd seen all of the wonders in the world. I'd been to Great Britain, Italy, Spain, Africa, and spots that didn't even appear on the map. I'd spent time around creatures that could kill me, but a wolf had never been one of them.

Looking at Embry, I was having a hard time believing she wasn't human. She didn't scare me. She didn't remind me of an animal. She was just her.

"Oh, my God. You let a wolf shifter pick me up from the airport!" I shouted the sudden realization.

"And you impressed him, so good on you. Vaughn gave me his approval the moment he opened your door. That's something he doesn't give a lot of people, but I'd already known I'd chosen my best friend well," she replied proudly.

"Who is he?" I asked.

"He's the pack beta. Second only to Roman. He serves our people and would die for any one of them, but earning his respect is a totally different thing. You should be proud."

I snorted. "I should be proud of impressing a *wolf shifter*?"

Embry turned to face me head-on and grabbed my forearms. "I know this is a lot. I also know none of this has really sunk in for you yet. At some point, likely soon, you're going to realize everything I've said is true. You might think you believe it now, but a part of you still thinks this is a bad dream or a joke. Just promise me that you won't run when it all sinks in. I meant it earlier. You're my best friend, and having you here is something I never thought could happen. I won't let anything take you away from me unless you truly don't want to be here."

Her speech made me question everything again. Embry was normally carefree and joyous. It was why I enjoyed her friendship so much. She made the hurt from missing my mother dull to a more manageable level.

Yet, even if all of this was real—a fact I was sure I couldn't ever forget—did I really want to hang around and have wolves be part of my life? I could just as easily catch the next flight out of the country and continue on as I had the last few years.

"Don't think too hard on things yet. Give me a week. Let me show you this isn't as bad as it may sound. Even if we don't know what that mark is, nothing will happen to you here," Embry said, full of confidence.

She stood up and set our untouched glasses back on the table. "Come on. I want to show you my home."

"Eh, I don't think that's a good idea. I'd rather stay right here and ask more questions," I said, leaning back into the couch.

Embry laughed. "Fat chance, woman. Get your ass up. I asked for a week, and I'm going to use every hour of it."

"But I'm tired. Can't I sleep for a while? I don't even know what time it is," I said, not lying. I knew if I had a comfortable bed, I'd be out within minutes.

"It's after three in the afternoon. You can't sleep now, or the jetlag will only get worse. I'll let you sleep after dinner. Now, come on."

She grabbed onto my hand and yanked me up from the couch with little effort. "You're really strong," I muttered.

"Wolf perks. I wonder if you'll get those. Accelerated healing, speed, increased appetite, stamina. All kinds of things humans could never dream of being capable of," Embry said as we walked out her door.

I ignored her, choosing to focus on our surroundings. I'd always thought Texas was a hot desert-type of state, but the area where Embry lived was green and lush, reminding me a lot of Oregon except the humidity was more extreme here.

Embry started chatting about her favorite things to do when she wasn't working, but she lost my attention as three wolves appeared in the clearing just beyond her house. Not normal-sized wolves. No, these ones were pushing four feet tall on all fours and built solid, not gangly like the only ones I'd ever seen.

I stopped moving, taking backward steps to the house. I couldn't do this. Seeing them was too much. Knowing my best friend turned into one was mind-blowing. I needed to get out of there.

"Cait?" Embry turned back to me, then followed my stare. "They're friendly. We have around three hundred wolves in our territory. Though, a lot of them don't live in this pack. There are smaller pockets Roman is also in charge of over the eastside of Texas. You won't find trouble with any of them, as I've already said."

She was trying really hard to make me not afraid, but words couldn't touch what my eyes were seeing. The wolves lowered their heads and kept their gazes on me as I stumbled back.

"I can't do this, Embry," I whispered once I was pressed against her door.

She grabbed my shoulders and shook me until I was forced to meet her stare. "You are Cait Mother Fuckin' Jones. You *can* handle this. I don't believe for one second that you're not strong enough to accept what you're going to see here. I will beat you if I have to, to show you what I know you're capable of handling."

Her words had already done the beating she threatened on about. I glanced back at the wolves. The longer I looked at them, the more they looked like overgrown dogs than man-eating animals. One was light grey with a few black spots, the other dark brown, and the third was a light tan, almost white, with brown paws. Their tongues hung out of their mouths as they seemed to wait for us.

"There you go. One thing at a time. You got this," Embry added when I relaxed under her grasp.

"Right. One thing at a time," I repeated.

"Now let's go say hello to James, Brad, and Ginger."

She said their names as if it would make them any less wolfy to me.

"If one of them bites me, I'm unfriending you," I grumbled as she laughed and pulled me along.

"That might have held more of a threat before you arrived here, but now that I've got you, I'm never letting you leave me," Embry said with a smile.

Her words packed an emotional punch that went straight to the center of my heart.

So much love for her.

Regardless, something told me that by the end of the day, a part of me was going to regret replying to her ridiculous comment all those years ago in that book group.

5

CAIT

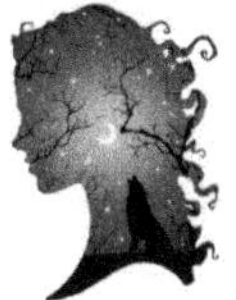

Two of the three shifters had paused to say hello —likely more curious than friendly. Mostly, I'd been surprised when they changed to their human forms fully dressed.

"Why weren't they naked when they shifted? Is it some kind of magic?" I asked once we walked away from the others. I heard a snort from behind us and turned to see Brad and Ginger snickering, but far enough away that they shouldn't have heard me.

"Umm, not magic like you might think, but a little yes. As long as we remember to think about our clothes, they don't get ruined in a shift. We also have excellent hearing." She grimaced as I blushed. The others had heard me.

"I thought that was a vampire thing," I whispered even though the two wolves were no longer in sight. I was also fully aware that my only knowledge of the supernatural came from fictional books.

"Well, them too. We have a lot of the same offensive traits as the blood suckers," Embry replied dryly.

"Do you not get along with them?" I asked.

She shrugged. "Depends on the nest and the pack. Some of us do, some don't. There is another territory in West Texas that is very old-school in their ways."

I read between the lines and was glad the few people I'd met at this pack weren't assholes like I took the "old-school" comment to mean.

Embry's home wasn't far from the pack house, and we didn't pass any other wolves that I could tell through the surrounding trees. We traveled down a dirt path in silence as I took in the tranquility of their land.

In all the travels I'd done the last few years since I'd lost my mother, there hadn't been too many places that were quiet enough I could hear my soul, but this was another I could add to that list.

At first, it was weird to think I could *hear* my soul, but after a few incidents, I was convinced that was what I sensed. The sound wasn't made from words or hums, but something else I'd yet to identify. Something tangible I could feel and hear. It was hard to describe. I'd thought it was my mom's spirit on a couple of occasions, but as I continued traveling and attempted to find myself, I knew it was all me.

Embry and I arrived back at the pack house, and she took us around the rear side of the massive structure that stretched even further back than I realized when first arriving.

"What is this?" I asked, pointing to fogged-up windows.

"Ramona's garden. Her pride and joy after Roman. Want to see inside? She keeps it in a greenhouse since the weather is so hot. That way, she can control things a bit more, or so she says."

I began to say yes, but my words were drowned out by the sound of exhaust.

Embry sighed. "That would be Vaughn. He's waiting on us, but I promise I'll give you a proper tour by the end of the day." She grabbed my hand, and I nearly tripped over my own feet after she jerked hard on my arm.

The back side of the house had a matching porch to the front, except instead of red double doors, there were sliding glass doors spanning the bottom floor and large windows covering the top. Suddenly, I wanted to be inside the house more than anything else just so I could see the view from the second floor.

We continued on after I was done gawking at the oversized home and my eyes landed on a cabin similar to Embry's, just slightly bigger and with a small garage attached to it. Vaughn was sitting on his bike, leather jacket still on and a grin plastered to his face.

"Lovely ladies." He nodded at each of us before meeting my gaze. "How are you liking our home so far?"

"Well, besides the angry welcome and seeing werewolves for the first time, I'd say it's been more than

I would have imagined if I'd known where I was coming," I replied.

Vaughn threw his head back and laughed before hopping off the bike. He threw an arm around me. "I like you."

Something snapped behind us, and when I tried to turn around, Vaughn's hold tightened. "How about I help with the tour? It's why I called Embry over here."

My brow pinched. I'd been with Embry since arriving. I hadn't once heard him call her, and I didn't even see her phone around.

Embry looped her arm through mine, pulling me out of Vaughn's hold, and tapped her mind. "Mind-speak. Something very few other supernaturals can do."

"You can hear each other's thoughts?" I gaped.

"Only when projected. We can't listen to each other when not invited. Well, all of us except for Roman. Though, he only does that if there is no other choice," Embry answered as Vaughn pulled his bike out of the way and revealed a UTV.

"What does that mean? No other choice?" I asked.

Embry hopped into the back of the off-road vehicle, and Vaughn pointed for me to sit in the front before speaking. "Our problems are like human problems. Sometimes alphas have to go to extreme measures for the greater good of the pack. Forcing their way into the wolves' minds is rare, but sometimes necessary.

"Roman might have been upset, but you have to remember, your existence was pretty much a fable before today. He had no idea what you were when the two of you crossed paths. He's a good alpha. Don't judge him based on your first impression."

"Or the second," Embry added with a smirk.

I nodded, unsure of how to respond. What did it matter what I thought of Roman? Sure, it sounded like Embry wanted me to stay, but I wasn't one of them. I didn't belong here. I doubted there would be too many more impressions I had to worry about with Roman.

Vaughn started the UTV, took off down the dirt path behind his house, and passed by a bigger garage that was detached from the main house.

"There are five main paths through the pack lands. If you get lost, find one of them and follow the sun back to the house. Don't knock on random cabins. That might get you killed. The people here are nice, but they like their privacy."

"How many… *people* are there?" The word "people" was weird to use when I knew they weren't human.

"This particular pack has between one hundred and one-hundred-fifty shifters at any given time. Currently, we have one-hundred-thirty-seven of them registered. All of them have homes here that they've built themselves or inherited. We don't force anyone to stay, but they can't give their spot away, either. We are very selective about the wolves we let in," Vaughn answered.

Embry pointed above my left shoulder. "See? Cabins everywhere."

"Okay, so five paths where I might get lost if I can't see the sun and cabins I shouldn't go to. This tour is off to a great start," I deadpanned.

This was a horrible idea. I never should have left Embry's house. I needed weeks to process all the new things I was learning, but neither of the two beside me seemed to care. They just kept spitting information out left and right.

"Some of the paths intersect, like here. If we go left, it takes us to the river, right goes back toward the training field, then the pack house. Which should we take?" Embry asked.

I let out a yawn. "Right. We can take left another day if that's okay."

Embry's hand clasped over my shoulder and her rose-gold hair whipped around my face when she leaned closer. "Right. Jetlag. You're probably hungry, too. Let's stop by and see Ramona."

Seeing Ramona meant going to the main house—the one I saw Roman go into, and I was too tired to deal with another run-in with him. The way he'd asked about me like I wasn't standing right there after he'd gotten out of the car grated on my nerves even more as time passed.

"I'm not very hungry. Sleep will be good for now," I said as Vaughn growled loudly at someone passing us who looked a lot like him, beard and all.

"My cousin Graeme. He loves me," Vaughn said as his cousin flipped him off, then we continued on down the path.

"That's the training field." Embry nudged me and pointed right.

It was an open grass area with an obstacle course

that included monster tires, ropes, and a tower with three sides and a bell at the top. Before I could check out the contraptions attached to it, Vaughn was jerking the UTV in the opposite direction.

"That looked like... um..." I tried to find the right word without being rude.

"Fun? A rush? Adventurous?" Embry said.

"Uh, sure. All of that," I grumbled, making her laugh.

Vaughn glanced between the two of us. "Am I missing something?"

"Cait here doesn't like exercise." Embry grinned widely.

Vaughn's brows raised. "Ah, that's right. And you expect her to survive here?"

Embry hugged me from behind as Vaughn pulled to a stop. "She's going to thrive here. I know it. I've got that good intuition," she said.

"That you do, VP." Vaughn laughed as Embry tugged me from my seat. "I've got work to do here. See you pretties later," he added as we walked back toward the pack house.

"Why did he call you VP?" I asked.

Embry blushed. "Well, I might have left another part of my job out."

"And what would that be?"

She looped her arm through mine again, thankfully pulling me away from the house I had no desire to enter. "So, some wolves have special powers. It's pretty rare, and most of the time subtle or useless, but I'm pretty proud of mine considering it landed me the position of VP of accounting. I have what I like to call luck with money. Vaughn thinks it's intuition. Either way, I can take a thousand dollars and turn it into tens of thousands in the stock market. I run all of the pack finances."

"I should question that, but I've had enough weird for the day. Maybe tomorrow after I wake up, but one last question. Do you guys have normal jobs with… humans?" Damn that was weird to say out loud.

"No, the pack owns a mill and a lot of us work there. I oversee the accounting department. You could work there, too. Or watch the pups if that's still something that interests you." She said the last bit with a smirk.

Embry had tried to talk me out of taking the nanny gig. She'd been all for me traveling, but taking a real job, not so much. I should have listened to her.

"I see. Well, maybe I'll give you the remainder of my inheritance to use your luck on. I think it's the least you can do after bringing me to a pack of wolves."

She pinched me hard, and I yelped. "First, I didn't force you here. Second, you're still speaking like you're human." Embry lifted my wrist. "News flash, my friend. You're not."

"You're an asshole," I said.

"But you love me."

That I did.

We arrived back at her place, and Ramona was just walking out of Embry's house. She waved, smiling brightly. She had short blonde-grey hair, umber eyes that shined under the filtering sunlight, and a warmth about her that made the lingering tension leave my body.

"Hi, ladies. I thought our guest might be hungry. I put leftover lunch on the counter." Ramona smiled at both of us.

"Thank you. That was very kind of you," I said first.

"I'm sorry about your welcoming. That's not normally how we treat guests. I want you to know that you're welcome inside the main house at any time. My son will be on his best behavior," Ramona said confidently.

"Alpha Momma always gets what she wants. If she says Roman will be nice, then he will be," Embry added, seeming to enjoy the situation a little too much.

Ramona smiled and moved to walk past us, then grabbed my arm gently. "May I see it?"

For a moment, I was confused, then lifted my wrist.

She sucked in a breath, tickling her fingers over the mark. "So much power within you, dear. You're going to be quite the treat around here if you choose to stay."

Ramona walked away, leaving my mind whirling more than ever before.

"Em?" My hands were shaking as she led me inside.

"You've been through hell already, Cait. You can handle whatever is coming next."

I laughed nervously. "You keep saying that."

"And I'll do it as many times as it takes for you to believe it. Now come on. Ramona makes the best food. Let's go see what she brought over."

Food and sleep. Then, it would be time for me to ask all the right questions. The afternoon had been more about observing the area and trying to convince myself I wasn't dreaming. Tomorrow would be more about action, if I could get past the fact that the people that I needed to get answers from turned into oversized dogs.

6

ROMAN

Ever since I saw that vixen on the beach, my senses had been completely thrown off. My smell, speed, and reactions—they'd all been acting erratically. I'd hoped when I got home things would get back to normal.

Unfortunately, that didn't happen.

After speaking with my parents, I took off into the woods and to my cabin. It wasn't as far from the pack house as I would have liked, but nobody bothered me there unless it was an emergency. I'd hoped to be by myself this week. Hoped to be in my wolf form, letting him distract me from things that shouldn't bother me any longer.

Yet, none of that was going to happen.

Instead, I was going to be left stressing about the past *and* the future.

You place blame where it doesn't belong, Roman, my wolf said.

If not with me, then with who?

With the wolf who challenged you. He had no business coming to our pack to take what wasn't his. We were too strong for him, and he knew it. This was not on us.

I scoffed. *That might be mostly true, but we could have let him live. We should have found a way. Instead, we're stuck with this guilt.*

My wolf grumbled. *No, you are, and you need to get over it.*

He was a bossy bastard.

Only a couple months after my father passed his alpha powers to me, I was challenged for ownership of our pack by another wolf from the West territory.

Alpha challenges weren't common practice nowadays. If an alpha potential wolf had an issue with the leadership, they left. Some wolves followed and started a new pack elsewhere. Most stayed behind. It was easy and kept the peace between our kind.

For too long, our ancestors were at war with each other. Families destroyed. Homes decimated. All of it pointless.

Not that I didn't enjoy being alpha, but I'd never have fought for the position if it wasn't already meant for me.

We are exactly where we belong, my wolf said confidently as I threw a rock into the river, watching it skip several times across the clear water.

The area around us was quiet. Only the birds and small prey lingered around the area. While the past had been heavy on my mind with the anniversary of when

I'd killed the young wolf the following day, I couldn't shake the face of one human woman that I shouldn't want or think about.

Except, ever since fleeing the beach, I smelled her on me. I heard her snarky voice. Laughed at how she stood up to me, showing a bravery few ever could under my alpha power.

All of that would have been heaven if only she wasn't human.

She's not and you know it. You're just too scared to admit it, my wolf added.

Shut it.

He laughed. *Make me.*

The wolf knew I couldn't. He'd been in my mind since the day I was born. My first friend and confidant, but that didn't mean he didn't annoy the hell out of me on occasion.

We need her, he added somberly.

I threw another rock, this time skipping the water all together and enjoying the thud as it landed in the bark of a tree.

I didn't want to need this woman. She couldn't be my equal. The other wolves would never respect a human-born as my mate. Even if she wasn't human any longer, she was still closer to that than wolf. I had been repeating these things in my head ever since I learned she wasn't a witch, but every time I did, my resolve weakened instead of getting stronger.

There wasn't much we knew about the Moon Goddess. She'd stayed out of our business for centuries.

The fact that she was dabbling in it now bothered me almost as much as having a human mate.

Not human, my wolf kindly reminded me. Again.

I snarled and ran a hand through my hair. Son of a bitch. Why did it have to be so damn complicated?

Shift and I can take care of the situation.

I laughed. *What are you going to do? She isn't a wolf. You can't talk to her.*

How do we know that? She might have one hiding away within her and we just need to draw the sensual being out.

Sensual, huh? Who are you and what have you done with my wolf? I asked.

I know this is hard for you to accept. You wanted a warrior, and you think that isn't what you've received, but I've met our creator. She isn't an evil being. She promised me a mate worth waiting for. I've been through many centuries alone. I believe Cait is worthy, and we need to give her the chance to prove herself. Not to us, but to the others.

Damn it. My wolf's pain from being alone for so long seeped through my mind and ached into my chest. My hands fisted at my sides as my canines extended. The shift was close. My wolf wanted control. He wanted his mate, but he was waiting on me—a very selfish me.

My wolf backed down, retreating from my mind and giving me time to think on my own again. I'd been out at the cabin for a few hours, but it wasn't long enough. It would never be long enough.

A mate. I had a damn mate.

The piece I'd been missing in my life. The piece I

didn't expect to find for several more decades but had stumbled upon by accident.

Or was it?

"Moon Goddess, what have you done and what is coming?" I asked, looking up into the cloudless, bright sky.

No answer came, not that I expected one.

Instead, the pull to return to the pack house grew stronger. I wanted days out in my spot, but I wasn't stubborn enough to do so. I needed to face whatever waited for me. My wolves needed to see me as the infallible alpha they trusted, and that was what I was going to give them.

I needed to listen to my wolf and trust that maybe he was right. Maybe Cait was more than she looked like on the outside.

Gods, I hoped so, because the more I thought about her, the more I wanted to wrap her in my arms and never let go. The draw of the mate bond was stronger than I ever believed, and the fact that she didn't seem affected by any of it drew me in even further if I was being honest with myself.

Go to her. Give her a chance, my wolf said.

And if she doesn't give us one? I asked.

My wolf angered, causing claws to extend from my fingers and fangs to cut my lip as a low growl rumbled through my body.

Easy, boy. If she's ours, we'll fight for her. We'll find a way to show her we're a worthy match.

With my words, he settled, but not entirely.

Apparently, my wolf was cockier than even I knew, because the thought of Cait rejecting us clearly hadn't been on his radar.

I went back inside the cabin and made sure everything was off. It wasn't much—just a smaller version of most of the others within the pack—but it was quiet. It was where I came to think, and it was perfect.

Closing the door behind me, I inhaled deeply. The scent of earth and trees heavily invaded my senses, but still, Cait's unique blend of flowers, citrus, and mint tickled beneath it all.

Gods, I didn't know how I was going to survive this woman. If her smell distracted me this badly, I couldn't imagine what tasting her would do to me.

She will only make us stronger, my wolf said, back to being his normal cocky self.

I sure as hell hope you're right.

Because if she didn't, there was more at risk than just losing a mate.

7

CAIT

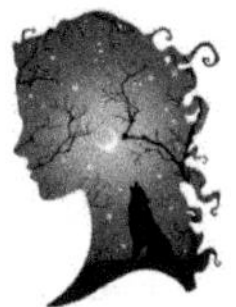

There was a bright light shining in my face, and everything was hot. My eyes burned and ached when I tried to open them. I pulled the pillow from behind my head and covered my face, but someone jerked it away.

"I don't think so, woman. Up. Now," Embry's voice demanded in my ear.

"Just let me sleep." I groaned. Jetlag was a bitch, and I hadn't gotten nearly enough rest.

"Dude. You've been out for eighteen hours. I didn't bring you here for me to still be bored."

My eyes opened, and I rubbed my face. "What?"

"Eight. Teen. Hours. Get up before you become a permanent part of the bed." Embry grabbed on to my wrist and yanked me up. A dizziness came over me as I stood, and she had to hold on to my shoulders.

"I'm going to be sick," I said.

"No, you're just starving. Let's get some food in you."

I slowly followed her out of the downstairs bedroom that she had announced was mine for as long as I'd have it. We were in the kitchen by the time I realized my t-shirt was twisted around my armpits, my butt was on display since I hated sleeping in shorts, and I likely had drool on my face, but none of that mattered when I smelled food.

A hunger like never before came over me and I practically dove for the counter, ramming two pieces of bacon into my mouth as I shoveled more food onto a plate.

As I was taking my third bite, a knock sounded at the door and panic set in. I took one step in hopes of running back to the bedroom, but it was too late. The door opened, and I was frozen in the kitchen, still wearing just an old shirt and underwear with Embry behind me, laughing her ass off.

"Good morning, Roman. Or is it afternoon? Either way, it's great, isn't it?" Embry beamed when I twisted to glare at her.

Daring a glance, I turned toward the door. Roman's eyes were locked on my bare legs, and my body flushed. The intensity of his stare nearly knocked me on my ass. Sense came over me, though, and I tugged my shirt down, hoping he couldn't see much.

"Did you need something?" Embry asked him, still grinning.

Roman cleared his throat as his eyes traveled from

my legs to my face before darting to Embry. "Ramona asked me to come check on the quarterly report for the mill."

"Funny. I emailed that to her yesterday evening. Must have gone to spam. I'll send it again," Em replied.

Roman glowered. "Must have." He reached for the door while looking at me. Our eyes locked, and I had to grip the counter as warmth moved through my chest, then straight to my wrist.

"I hope you're finding our pack welcoming, Cait," Roman said, the words sounding stiff.

I managed to nod at him, enjoying that he had a hard time keeping his gaze on my face and not my legs.

He grunted and slid out the door before I could blink.

I fell onto the stool at the counter and was no longer hungry for food. Roman was… I didn't know what he was, but there was something about him that overwhelmed my senses. Even back on the beach, there had been a draw about him I hadn't missed.

"Well, that was fun," Embry said, shoving my plate closer. "Eat."

When I didn't pick up the fork, she waved a piece of bacon against my lips until I snatched it. "Fine. Thank you for breakfast, or brunch," I said, forcing down the food in hopes of getting that man out of my head.

"I think he likes you. It's cute," she said when I began chewing on the eggs.

I choked on the bite. "Excuse me? He's said one nice

thing to me, and I'm not even sure if he meant it. I hardly think that means he likes me."

"Wolf intuition. Roman is nervous around you. I can smell it. Don't get me wrong, he was plenty angry as well, but there was underlying curiosity that I could sense. I just don't know why you would have caught his attention."

I punched her. "Thanks, asshole."

She rubbed her arm. "No, that came out wrong. I just mean, you're not a wolf. Our kind don't usually look twice at other supernaturals, let alone humans, but I guess if you have the mark, then it makes you like us. I just wonder if you were ever human."

My wrist still throbbed, but it was easy to ignore when I kept my mind busy. Turning my hand, I rubbed my fingers over the crescent shape. "What does all of this mean, Em?"

I'd done my best to avoid the heavier topics on my first day here. It had been a lot to take in, learning wolf shifters were real and being told I was marked by their queen or whatever she was. After too much sleep, I was ready for answers. Ones I hoped I could handle.

"How about you finish eating and shower first? I'll go see Ramona and ask her to come over. She really wants to be part of this conversation."

"Why?" I asked.

Embry shrugged. "I don't ask a lot of questions. It's not in my nature. While Ramona's mate might not be the alpha anymore, she is still the alpha female of our pack—until Roman takes a mate—and has my respect."

The inner workings of this world were going to be hell to learn, but I couldn't deny I was intrigued. Embry climbed the stairs to her loft, and I hurried to finish eating.

Once I was done, I headed into the bathroom to find all my toiletries were already at home on the shelves. My heart warmed. Embry really was the best friend. It didn't matter that she had an animal inside her that could kill me. She had a heart of gold that had gotten me through more hell than I cared to recount.

As soon as the water was hot, I rushed through a shower and padded out into the short hallway in just a towel. A growl rumbled from behind me, and it sounded like the front door clicked shut as I turned around.

"Embry?" I called as my heart raced.

No reply.

She had said she was going to get Ramona. Did someone know I was in the house alone? Were they coming to…? I didn't know what they might do, but either way, I was scared out of my mind. I ran toward the door and flipped the deadbolt into place before peeking out the window.

Nothing that I could see was out there besides trees, grass, and the dirt path. I tried to steady my breathing as I leaned against the wall, but by the time I thought maybe I'd just been hearing things, the door handle started to rattle, making me scream.

"Cait?" Embry called, and the door cracked with impact.

"I'm okay. Hold on!" I yelled through the wall as I unlocked the deadbolt.

"What the hell, dude?" she demanded, gathering me into her arms as Ramona pushed in behind us.

"Sorry. I thought someone had come in while I was in the shower, so I locked the door, then began to panic. I'm sure it was nothing," I said.

Embry met Ramona's eyes, and the older woman nodded at her.

"What?" I asked.

"Uh, nothing. Go get dressed so we can chat," Embry said, shoving me toward my room.

Wolves were weird creatures. Strong and scary, but weird, nonetheless.

Even my clothes were hung up and folded into the drawers already. Embry had been busy while I slept like the dead. I grabbed jean shorts and a yellow tank top. It was August. In Texas. I was going to melt in anything else.

Grabbing a brush from the bathroom, I went into the living room where Embry and Ramona waited with snacks and orange juice.

I brushed through my wet strands while standing. "So, what am I?" I asked first, because not much else mattered until I knew that and what it meant for my future.

Ramona chuckled. "I like you."

I didn't reply. I didn't know what to say without offending her, because she didn't know me. How could she like me other than for the fact that I was probably entertainment to them? The poor pathetic human scared of all the big bad wolves. Well, after the door episode, I needed to own my fear and embrace whatever courage I could muster if I wanted answers.

"I know you don't know me, but Embry has told me a lot about you, so I apologize if I act like I know you. I feel I already do, but I'm also excited to learn about you from *you* instead of someone else," Ramona added, making me feel like a first-class jerk.

"Oh. Well, there isn't much to get to know," I said, putting my brush down and taking a seat across from them in a chair.

Ramona grinned in a motherly way. "I doubt that, but let me answer your question. You are Luna Marked. You were born human to human parents. Everything you know about your life is true, but our creator seemed to see something in you. She has blessed you with the mark of our kind."

Blessed? I wasn't sure I would use that word, but I didn't want to be rude, so I kept my mouth shut.

"What does that mean, though? Am I going to become a wolf?" I asked, not really ready for that answer, but I knew I needed to know.

Embry sighed and spoke first. "This is the part we're not really sure about. You don't have a wolf spirit, and the history books don't say much about your kind other than only the strongest of humans are chosen. A human with purpose and pure intention. One who will protect our kind no matter the cost."

I laughed. "*I'm* supposed to protect *you*? That's

hilarious. Seriously, though, what does this mark mean? Why does it burn and pulse like it's alive?"

"We don't have all of the answers for you yet, but we're working on them. I thought maybe for today that we could give you the basics about pack life and see what questions you have for us about staying here," Ramona said, her eyes soft and filled with care.

"So, you're saying you know what I am, but not what I will be or what I can do?" I asked, looking at Embry. She could never lie to me without turning her stare away.

Her pale blue eyes stayed on mine, and I breathed a sigh of relief. "Not yet, but I promise we will."

"Good enough for now, I guess," I replied, even though it really wasn't. Thinking back to something Embry had said, I decided to see what other information I could get. "What is a wolf spirit?"

Ramona beamed, likely happy to be on a subject that she seemed familiar with. "A wolf spirit is something all of us shifters have. It's like having your best friend with you at all times. Our wolves have their own voice and feelings. They live many lifetimes until the Moon Goddess grants them peace in the afterlife. So far, my wolf has been through six life cycles, four of which have been with her mate, my husband."

My eyes widened. Holy shit, that was weird. I tried to imagine having another person inside me. One who had lived lifetimes before me. It wasn't easy.

"And you have this spirit, too?" I asked Embry just

to be sure, even though she'd already mentioned something about her wolf liking me.

She nodded. "Mine is on her third life and was with her mate last time, so we hope to find him again, but it doesn't always work out that way."

There was a sadness in Embry's voice, and I wondered if that came from her or the wolf. Probably both. My heart ached for her loneliness.

"Since I don't have a wolf spirit, will I have a mate? I'm not certain how comfortable I am with that," I said. The thought of having someone predestined for me was weird, but if I was able to keep an open mind, maybe it wouldn't be so bad, depending on the situation. Only maybe, though.

Embry smiled at me with happiness radiating from her. "I hope so. It would mean you'd stick around longer."

Ramona cleared her throat and continued, "So, wolves have spirits and mates. We can shift whenever we want but are never stronger than during a new moon."

I held my hand up. "New moon? I thought it was a full moon."

They both laughed. "You'll find some similarities about us in books and movies, but most of them are either opposite to what's true or slightly off as not to give our kind away. We enjoy interacting with the humans, but they aren't ready to know about us," Ramona answered.

"What else?" I asked, feeling bad for cutting her off.

Embry held up her snack plate. "We eat. A lot. Our metabolism burns through food and alcohol pretty quickly. We age slower than humans, and we can live around five hundred years. You'll find that those of us who go in public can only do so in the same area for a few decades. The staff at the mill changes frequently because of that."

I gulped. Five hundred years. That was more than I expected. A lot more.

"How old are you two?" I asked.

"I really am twenty-three," Embry answered.

"I'm eighty-four," Ramona said, and I choked on air.

She maybe looked forty. I couldn't believe it.

Embry laughed. "Soon enough, this will all seem normal to you. I promise."

My best friend might have believed she was telling the truth, but something told me that was far from the case.

8

CAIT

After our chat, Ramona excused herself and I hoped to spend the rest of the day in the cabin with Embry. Except, she had other plans.

"So, now that you know a little more about us, do you feel more comfortable going out?" she asked.

"We did that yesterday," I replied.

"No, we took you on a ten-minute drive to warm you up to the area. That was nothing. Our lands stretch for hundreds of miles. The property we're on is our main pack, but we own sections up and down the eastern side of Texas," she said.

"So, you want to go on a road trip?" That I could probably get on board with.

"No, I want to take you to the river. It's over a hundred degrees outside and humid as hell. I want to swim. It's something I do a lot on my days off," she replied, and a wave of sadness came over me that I didn't already know that. I wondered how many more things I'd learn about Embry that I thought I already knew.

I chose not to worry about it then, though. A dip in the water did sound like fun. I missed the Australian ocean waters already. Even if a river wouldn't be anywhere near the same, maybe it would bring back memories from the one I used to frequent back in Oregon as a kid.

"Okay, let's do it," I said.

Embry gaped. "Seriously? I don't have to drag you out of here screaming? I thought you'd fight leaving the house. I'm disappointed, actually."

She had a point. A part of me did want to forever stay locked away from potential dangers, but I couldn't be scared of what I didn't know. If I had to be here for a while in order to figure out what I was, then I needed to get comfortable with the wolves. At least from a moderate distance.

Embry was already headed upstairs to change, so I did the same. By the time I was done, she was standing in front of the open door and holding a beach bag with a glowing smile. "Ready?"

"Under one condition. When I'm ready to go, please don't make a scene. Let's just go," I said.

"As long as you've given it a real chance, then yes, I agree," she replied, and I nodded.

Embry was the only person I had left that I considered family. As scared as I was, I had a feeling if I wanted to keep her as my best friend, then I needed to figure out how to be part of her world. I had to do this.

We walked the dirt path toward the pack house again. "Vaughn is giving me his UTV for us to use for however long we need. We just need to stop and get it."

Realization set in before I asked how she'd manage to set that up with Vaughn. I had to admit, I was slightly jealous of their wolf telepathy tricks.

Embry waved at others as we made our way to Vaughn's. Each of the people we passed smiled at her and stared, confused, at me. Something that hopefully wouldn't last for long. I wasn't a fan of the attention.

The UTV was already out of the garage and waiting for us. Embry hopped onto the driver's seat, and I got in next to her. She slammed her foot down on the gas and nearly gave me whiplash.

"Dude. Are you in a hurry?" I grumbled.

She laughed. "Vaughn is obsessed with his toys. He doesn't often share, and I don't own one because I normally run everywhere with my wolf. I've been dying to drive this beast." Her hands roamed over the wheel as we flew down the path.

There would be no sightseeing today.

Her mention of her wolf made me feel bad. "Are you suffering by spending so much time with me and not your wolf?" I wasn't sure how that worked and didn't want to be selfish.

"Nah. I went out while you were sleeping. She understands, and I'll get out again tonight. When you're ready, I'll shift in front of you. She'd like to meet you."

"I think I'd like that, too." I meant what I said from

the bottom of my heart. Even though they were simple words, I hoped Embry understood how important she was to me. She was all I had left, and I wanted her to be herself around me.

Within fifteen minutes, we arrived at a beach area. There were benches and barbecues set up, a volleyball area, and horseshoes. Oh, and about thirty freaking wolf shifters.

Every one of them turned toward us when Embry parked, kicking up a bunch of sand. She waved animatedly while I shrank down into my seat.

Embry leveled her stare on me. "You promised."

"You left out that there would be dozens of people here. Given there are only one-hundred-thirty-something people living here, I assumed maybe just a handful."

"You know what assuming usually means, right? Plus, nobody is going to hurt you. I doubt if anyone will even talk to you," she said, and I grimaced. That did *not* make me feel any better.

I slid out of the seat and hurried around to Embry's side. Damn, I hated feeling so out of my skin. I'd traveled through foreign countries for multiple years and handled myself just fine. People could be monsters, too, but apparently, it was scarier when I knew what kind of monster lay beneath the surface.

Guilt instantly kicked me in the gut. I was being an asshole by judging them before I even gave them a chance. It shouldn't matter that they turned into wolves. They were part human as well. They looked and acted like it anyway. I needed to focus on that.

Embry took my hand and led us toward an empty spot on the sandy beach. The river was wide and calm. Kids and adults played in the water and on the beach. Families built sandcastles and cooked meals. If I'd arrived here without knowing it was a wolf pack, I'd have never known they were any different than me.

I could do this. Supernaturals weren't scary. I was safe. Everything was fine.

Embry tugged her shorts and shirt off, and I followed. We jumped into the water, and I sighed in relief as the cool liquid relaxed my sore muscles. I dipped my head back and closed my eyes, floating on the water's surface until Embry decided to dunk me.

Her action started a war between the two of us and others soon joined in. We were beating each other with water noodles and being tossed around. I laughed and screamed and had a blast, completely forgetting my reality for a while.

Everything was going great until my wrist started burning as one of the other wolves tried to pick me up. As he did, my mark must have done something to set him off, because he snarled in my face, showing fangs I could have gone my whole life without seeing.

"What was that for, freak?" he snarled at me.

Embry was between us in one second. "Whoa, Blake. What's going on?"

"She burned me. Maybe she *is* a witch like the others are saying," he spat.

The mark was throbbing again and the hairs on the back of my neck stood.

Blake tried to get in my personal space, but Embry blocked him. "She didn't mean to hurt you. You can smell her fear. Calm down, man. We were having fun."

Blake never once took his dark eyes off me. "Yeah, I can smell the fear, and it's making me hungry."

Something—or someone—was moving at impossible speeds toward us. As I stepped out of the way, Blake was flung ten feet across the water. Tension released from me, and I believed the danger was gone until I was thrown over the shoulder of someone I couldn't see.

"Shit," Embry said as I fought to get free. "You're going to be fine, Cait. I promise!"

What the hell did that mean?

"Let me down," I screamed as I beat on the muscled back of the man carrying me. He was fully dressed, the cotton clinging tightly to his warm skin. Why he'd even been at the beach made no sense to me. My wrist burned every time I hit him, and my movements only seemed to be hurting me, so I saved my energy.

Once I stopped fighting and started paying attention to my surroundings again, I found we were in the forest, away from the crowds, and my body was pulsating with energy.

"Where are you taking me?" I demanded, hoping I wasn't going to have to haunt Embry in my afterlife if this dude killed me.

He grunted.

"Are you incapable of words?" I asked, because why not poke the wolf, right?

"He hurt you." The words were clipped and full of rage, his voice masked by the emotions.

"Technically, I hurt him. Plus, Embry was right there. I would have been just fine without your interference, so if you wouldn't mind taking me back, that'd be great," I said, having little hope my words would work.

Instead of responding, the guy dropped me to my feet, and I stepped back against a big rock. I pressed my hands against the moss-covered stone and looked up at my kidnapper. "Seriously? You again?"

Roman stood before me, and his blue eyes sparked with flecks of silver. His arms boxed me in, and he lowered his head to mine. The closer he got to me, the calmer he became.

"Are you okay?" he asked quietly.

This guy had mental problems. He was furious, then nice, then psycho, and now concerned. I didn't get it.

"I'm fine. I'd like to go back to Embry," I said, keeping my head held high. I didn't want to show him any fear, though according to the conversation between Embry and the Blake guy, Roman would be able to smell it anyway. Creepy as hell.

"I'm sorry, Cait. I didn't mean to scare you. It's just, you…"

"I what?" I asked as he closed his eyes.

When they opened back up, the intensity of his gaze had my knees going weak. I held on tighter to the rock behind me and tried to even my breathing. Why did I want his lips on me so badly?

"I can't let anything happen to you," he whispered while moving closer to me. The heat from his body singed my skin, and the mark on my wrist was almost painful. It seemed to hurt the worst around him, and I had no idea why.

"Why do you care?" I asked, my words breathier than I liked, given his close proximity.

"I shouldn't," he replied, pausing as if he wanted to elaborate, but chose not to.

I couldn't tell if it was his words and actions that were confusing me or the smell of cut wood and heady spices suddenly invading all my senses that did it.

Roman's hand moved to my cheek, cradling my face. His touch burned a fire through me that I knew I should run from, but instead, ached to be closer to. I'd lost all control over my actions the moment he touched me.

"What are you doing to me?" I asked, closing my eyes with a defeated sigh.

This was not me. I didn't swoon for guys. I didn't let them touch me like they owned me. Except there wasn't a single part of me that wanted him to stop.

"Something I should fight, but I'm not strong enough to," he whispered right before kissing my forehead and then the cheek he wasn't holding.

I opened my eyes, heart beating out of my chest, and could barely stand on my own. "How is this happening?" I asked, assuming he knew why I was ready to throw every caution to the wayside and throw myself at him.

Crap, this was not me.

There was a battle going on in his eyes. Whatever he had to say, he didn't want to. Wrinkles formed between his brow, and a frown deepened around his lips. I itched to touch him and make him smile again. Yet, I had no clue why. I tried to fight what was happening to me, but it felt too good to back away from.

Roman seemed to come to the same conclusion as he moved closer to me and whispered, "You're mine, Cait. The other half of my soul."

Instead of feeling better at understanding what was happening, his words were like ice water being dumped over my head. I tensed within his hold, remembering the conversation I'd just had with Ramona and Embry. Had they known? Did Embry keep this from me? I was going to kill her if so.

Roman backed up a pace. "I'm sorry. I didn't mean to upset you."

His jaw was tense, and his hands were fisted at his sides while he watched me. I didn't know what he was waiting for. I didn't know how I was supposed to respond to his words. I didn't have a wolf spirit. While I'd been mildly intrigued earlier about the concept of mates, having someone claim to be his didn't sit right with me.

Roman was looking at me like I already belonged to him, and a part of me loved that, but the stubborn side of my brain was screaming "hell no" at the thought. I couldn't belong to Roman's wolf if I didn't have one of my own.

"You're wrong. I'm not a wolf," I said, lifting my chin to stare him down while my chest rose and fell with anxiousness about what he would do next.

His lips fought a smile as he stayed where he was. "I know you're not. It's why I was angry before. I thought you were there to trick me, and I'm sorry for the way I reacted, but I know better now. My wolf knows, and I trust him with my life."

I was supposed to believe his wolf? Fat chance of that happening.

Out of nowhere, my wrist flared again, causing me to yelp as I cradled it to my chest, holding it tightly with my other hand. Roman was back in front of me within a split-second. "What's wrong?" he asked.

"Nothing. It's just the mark. It seems to have a mind of its own," I said, hissing as it got worse.

Roman pried my fingers open until I let go and he could see the mark for himself. "It's full of energy."

"Is that good or bad?" I asked.

He smiled at me. "Hopefully good." He lifted my arm and pressed his lips against the crescent shape. Relief was instantaneous, and I sighed, leaning my head on his shoulder against my better judgement.

His other hand wrapped around my hip, holding me close to him. "I will always take away your pain," he said softly.

Jesus. My heart swelled and ached over his words while my brain was fighting what was beginning to feel like a losing battle. I couldn't make sense of Roman. Everything about the situation was overwhelming me. I wanted to push away from him and get a clear head. I wanted to stand on my own. I wanted to take my own pain away.

Except his touch felt too damned good.

"I should get you back to the pack house. Embry is yelling at me." He grinned. "She must really love you, because she's never once disagreed with me. Well, at least not since we were kids."

"She's my best friend. We protect each other," I said.

Roman held my chin. "I can protect you, too."

My stomach dipped with nerves that had nothing to do with fear. Thankfully, he didn't expect a response. He picked me up, cradling me against his chest, and winked. "Hold on tight and we'll be back to her in under a minute."

Then, he ran as if there was a fire under his ass.

9

ROMAN

Telling Cait she was my mate wasn't something I'd planned. Actually, I'd been nervous as hell about the thought of saying the words. For other wolves, it wasn't necessary. Both sides just knew, but given Cait wasn't a wolf, I'd wondered how long I should wait.

After nearly being caught trying to visit Cait when I thought she was still sleeping, I'd waited until she and Embry left the house to get a better look at her. The draw to her was growing by the hour, and the alpha in me didn't like being so out of sorts, but I also knew a mate would never be a bad thing. I needed to see her.

They were headed to the lake. I almost didn't follow, trying to be respectable, but the pull was undeniable. I'd settled in, intent to just watch how the pack treated her for a few minutes, then leave them be. I thought maybe the others would ignore her or scare her. Instead, I was captured by the fact they'd let her join right in.

Embry likely had something to do with that, but she wasn't alpha. Maybe they sensed something about Cait.

Before I had let my mind mull over that thought, Blake was in Cait's face, and it didn't appear as if he was going to calm down on his own. I'd considered sending a command telepathically, but the rage building inside me at the thought of anyone laying hands on Cait needed a more physical reaction.

We should have torn the head from his body. He had no right to talk to our mate that way, my wolf seethed.

If I'd listened to my wolf, I would have, but I'd settled for slamming his body with so much force, he probably had some broken ribs. When he was far enough away and I was walking in the opposite direction with a freaked-out Cait, I'd made sure to let Blake know I'd be dealing with him more formally later.

I hadn't intended to take Cait away from Embry. I didn't even want her to know I'd been present, but things changed, and I wanted what I wanted. I was the alpha and needed my mate. There wasn't anything wrong with that.

Touching her, holding her, comforting her. It was more than I ever imagined it would be. The mark on her wrist held a power different to any wolf shifter I'd ever known. That made things much easier. If we could learn more about it and how to harness its energy, I wouldn't have to fear for Cait as I previously thought.

I thought I'd have to fight the growing need for her, especially after my wolf decided to continually push thoughts of her on to me. Saving her and being alone with her when I knew the truth made the idea of her as my mate easier to accept. Once I did that, the need to claim her grew with every passing second, something I had the bond to thank for.

I took Cait back to Embry after growing tired of the shifter trying to knock on the metaphorical door to my head. I didn't need to hear her words to know what she wanted, but Embry was on my time, and I'd only been ready to take Cait back when I knew she'd had too much. I hadn't expected her to care for Cait so much, and it made me feel better that Cait had someone she could trust here.

She might have craved my touch in the moment, but I saw the fight in her eyes. Cait wasn't going to accept me as quickly as I had her. A thought I tried to keep to myself considering how irate my wolf had gotten when I mentioned it before.

We will show her that we can provide for her and protect her like no one else in this world, my wolf said as we ran with Cait in my arms, conviction burning from his words.

Yes, my friend. We will.

Embry was waiting for us at the nearest path, leaning against the UTV. She was already dressed and holding a towel for Cait.

"Are you okay?" she asked Cait as soon as I slowed.

"Yeah, everything is fine," Cait replied but didn't seem sure of her words.

Embry pointed a finger at me. "She's my friend. *My*

best friend. You harm a hair on her head or a valve in her heart and I don't care if you're my alpha. I will gut you."

I let Cait down, holding her arms in case she wasn't steady after the run. Once I knew she was okay, I smiled at Embry, a shifter I hadn't expected to be so insubordinate. Normally, I'd do something about that, but this was a fragile situation.

"First, given that this is new territory for all of us, I'll ignore the threat you've given to your alpha, but make it a habit, and we might have to chat," I said, pausing for a moment to let my words sink in.

Embry nodded, knowing she'd stepped over the line, but there was a fire within her eyes that told me she'd do it again in a heartbeat just for Cait.

"Secondly, I didn't take Cait without reason. Blake had gotten too close to her," I added, even though I shouldn't have needed to give her an explanation.

Embry is your mate's best friend. She is going to be helpful in gaining Cait's trust. You're going to have to put up with things from Embry that you wouldn't from others, my wolf said, and I knew he was right. I'd already been thinking it myself.

Embry narrowed her icy eyes on me, and then they began to widen as she glanced between me and Cait. "Oh, my Gods. She's your… No. It's not possible."

"That's what I thought, but my wolf says otherwise," I said.

"Holy shit. Cait, are you okay?"

Cait nodded, still standing next to me even though I

wasn't holding on to her. I worried she wouldn't be affected by the bond, but she seemed to be, based on her earlier actions and the way she still gravitated toward me. This was something we could work with.

I watched her and grinned when she looked up at me. Her breath hitched and heart rate increased, something I rather enjoyed. "I'm sure you have a lot more questions. Ones you might not feel comfortable talking to me about yet, and I respect that. Finish your day with Embry, then have dinner with me tonight and I can explain more."

She glanced between me and Embry several times. "Uh, sure?" she replied, even though there really hadn't been a question in my statement.

I cradled her cheek once more and squeezed gently. "See you in a couple hours then."

Deciding it was better for me to leave first, I nodded at Embry and took off. I wasn't sure where I was going until I heard Vaughn's deep laughter and changed directions.

He was sitting on his front porch when I ran up. He nodded at me before lifting a glass of water to his mouth. "What's up, boss?"

"I told Cait she's my mate," I said and took a step back as Vaughn spit his drink everywhere.

"Come again? She's your what?"

"My. Mate," I said slower.

He ran a hand over his thick beard. "Well, I'll be damned. I knew I liked her. She was interesting during the car ride. Seems just the right amount of scared of our kind. The ones who are too eager to know about us tend to cause problems."

"Yeah, well, hopefully that fear goes away soon," I said, taking a seat beside him.

"Not to get all deep on you, but how are you feeling about a human mate?" he asked.

I knew Vaughn didn't really care about the details. He just wanted to make sure I was right in the head, which was a proper question as my beta. If Cait was going to be a distraction, Vaughn needed to be aware.

"At first, I was furious, as you saw. For so many reasons, but mostly because it scared the hell out of me. She's not like us. The pack. What if they don't accept her? The mark either hurt Blake today, or more likely took him by surprise. I'm sure that will make things more difficult."

"What do you mean hurt him?" Vaughn asked.

"I'm not sure. I didn't wait around long enough to ask questions before tossing Cait over my shoulder and getting her away from everyone else."

He whistled. "This could be a problem if the mark attracts the wrong kind of attention and word gets out. We already have enough to deal with from the west."

I glared at him. "I know that, but it's not like I can take it away from her. According to history books, the Moon Goddess 'blessed her' with it."

I'd never been so annoyed with lack of information about our wolf history. I'd searched through the library tower and there were only three books so far that mentioned the Moon Goddess. Two were just passing entries that meant nothing, and the third was in an ancient language that I hadn't had enough time to translate yet. I'd spend however long it took to figure out what Cait's mark meant.

"With the higher temperatures, I've got the super squads off duty from training. I have free time. Tell me how I can help," Vaughn said.

I sighed at his ridiculous name for wolves that were our pack's primary protectors, but let it go.

"We need to make sure nobody is talking. Even innocent words can have negative effects. Until we know more about this mark and what it means for Cait, we can't have the other packs finding out," I said.

"You know there's an easy way to do that as alpha, right?" Vaughn asked.

"Of course, I know. I just hate to use it. I don't want the pack to think I don't trust them when they've never given me reason not to." As alpha, I could force all of my wolves to keep the knowledge of Cait to themselves, but neither my father nor I had ever used that particular power. The thought of taking someone's will away never sat well with me.

Vaughn jumped up from his seat. "Well, it's time for me to go socialize."

"What?"

"If you want them to like Cait, someone has to campaign for her. Are *you* going to do it?" he asked.

I loved our pack, but I tried not to get too close. There was a fine line between keeping their respect and being their friend. I'd found a good balance between the two and had no desire to change the dynamics by talking up my mate.

"Exactly. I've spent the most time with her outside of Embry, so let me do it. The people adore me." Vaughn grinned, and I knew he was right.

"Fine. Go. And come see me when you're done. Unless it's dinner time. I'll be busy."

His brows waggled. "Going to be with your lady?"

"That's none of your business." I got up and walked away, keeping my smile hidden until he could no longer see my face.

"Just because I can't see it, doesn't mean I don't know you're happy as a tween at a boy band concert!" he called after me. I just shook my head, stuffing down my laughter.

I had more important things to concern myself with, like winning Cait over. I knew nothing about her, but I was going to do whatever it took to learn everything I could.

Kalynne.
KALYNNE_ART

10

CAIT

What in the ever-loving hell had just happened? Roman had held me in some sort of trance. He'd called me a witch when we first met, but I was pretty sure he was packing some juju of his own, because my blood burned with a need I'd never known, and my heart was about ready to give out.

The ride back to Embry's was filled with awkward silence. I tried to process what had transpired with Roman, but none of it was making sense.

When Embry parked the UTV in front of her door, I stayed in my seat, wrapped in the towel she'd given me.

She turned back to me, raising a brow. "Are you getting out?"

"Tell me I'm dreaming, Em. Tell me none of this is real," I said, hating to sound weak, but I couldn't deny how scared I was after what went down with Roman.

With every new piece of information, I felt like I was losing control, and that didn't sit well with me.

After losing my mom the way I did and not being able to do a damned thing about it, I'd avoided situations where there was too much out of my control. Yet, somehow, I'd ended up in the worst possible scenario that left me spiraling.

Embry was at my side in an instant, picking me up like I weighed nothing even though we were nearly the same size. "Come on, Cait. I've got something to help."

I fought against her hold, but her grip only tightened as we approached the door. She managed to hold me with one arm and open the door without missing a step, then kicked it closed as she dropped me on her couch. "Don't move," Embry demanded.

I landed with a thud, my teeth rattling as my head hit the back of the couch. I muttered a few choice words and straightened myself. I was a hot mess from being pulled out of the lake and not having done anything with my long strands. I leaned forward to go to the bathroom, but Embry growled at me.

"I said don't move!" Her voice echoed from the kitchen.

"I'm still in my swimsuit. I just need dry clothes and a brush," I yelled back, even though she wasn't that far from me.

Instead of responding, she leaped over the couch, holding two glasses and a dark bottle. "Your suit isn't wet anymore, and your hair is beyond help without a shower. You can wait. Now, tell me everything that happened, and not just today. I want you to repeat every moment with Roman since Australia."

Embry's eyes bored into me, and I sighed. She was like a dog with a bone. Except I was the bone, and I didn't like it.

Instead of wasting time arguing with her, I repeated what she wanted to know. This time, she asked more questions about the mark as I spoke and was intrigued from the first word to the last.

"I can't freaking believe it," she said when I finished.

"Believe what? What is happening to me, and how do I make it stop?" I asked, only slightly calmer than before.

"You're mated to the pack alpha. My best friend is mated to my alpha. This is the most awesome thing ever." Her grin was too big, and her excitement was too much for my panic.

"Embry, you're out of your damned mind. This is… I don't know what it is, but I'm not okay." My words finally registered with her, and she handed me a glass of amber liquid.

"Don't drink it too fast. It doesn't get wolves drunk, but it does loosen us up. It might put you on your ass," she added with a wink.

I took a sip and spit it out, just barely missing Embry's face. "That's horrid."

She laughed. "I guess it's an acquired taste."

"Seriously, Embry. Being told I have a mate is beyond anything I'm comfortable with. It was one thing to accept that my best friend turns into a wolf, but whatever happened back at the lake is a whole different scenario. One I'm no longer okay with." I held my wrist up. "This mark. Whatever it means. I don't want it."

Embry reached for me with one hand as the other set her drink down. "I know we don't have a lot of answers for you, but I promise you're safe here. Roman is a good man. He won't force anything on you that you don't want. Being mated doesn't mean… well, it doesn't mean anything bad."

I jerked my hand from her grip and stood, pacing in front of the couch and feeling exposed in so little clothing while having this emotional conversation. "Then, what the hell does it mean? I'm not a wolf. I'm human."

She stood and grabbed both of my shoulders, shaking me. "Calm down, Cait. I'm going to tell you something and I need you to hear it. No, not just hear, but really understand the words I say." She paused, and I took a deep breath. "You're *not* human. The moment that mark appeared on your wrist, your destiny changed. I know this is hard to accept, but it's the truth and I'll keep repeating it until the words stick."

Mother freaking hell. Tears pricked at my eyes, and my frustration was beyond controllable. My emotions were all over the place. As I held the stare of my best friend, I did my best to calm down as she requested.

"How is any of this even possible? Am I only mated to him because of the mark? What does it actually mean, other than I'm going crazy?" I asked once the tears dried up.

She tugged me toward the bathroom. "The how isn't easily explainable. You're new to our world, but some things don't have explanations. They just are what they are. Magic works in ways we can't always control."

"Magic? What does that have to do with anything?" I asked.

Embry turned on the shower. "We can't do spells or produce magic, but turning from human to wolf isn't natural. It's a power gifted to us by the Moon Goddess. Much like your mark."

I snorted and pointed at my wrist. "I wouldn't call *this* a gift."

Her face softened. "You say that now, but give it time. I believe I was drawn to you for a reason. I think you were meant for this world, and I'm going to make sure nothing happens to you. I promise you, Cait. You're my best friend. Now, get your ass in the shower."

She sat on the counter and waited.

"You're going to stay?" I asked with a grin I couldn't hold back.

"It's not like I don't have all the same stuff you've got going on under there. Plus, nudity isn't a big thing for shifters, and if I stay, we can kill two birds with one stone. You can quit smelling like fish water, and we can keep talking."

I shook my head at her, considering she'd been swimming in the same water, but let the slight go. Steam was already billowing from the water, so I undressed and pulled the curtain back.

After I rinsed my hair and began to wash up, I peeked at Embry. "What happened to the talking?"

She rolled her eyes, flicking back her rose-gold hair. "Well, I was waiting for you to ask more questions."

"You didn't answer all the ones from before. This thing with Roman. Why did I want him so badly when he was around, but now that feeling is gone?" I asked. Well, it was mostly gone. The memory of his touch seemed to be burned into my brain.

I stood under the spray of water, pulling at the knots in my hair as I waited for a reply.

"Really? The pull is gone? That's interesting. Normally when you find your mate, the attraction is hard to fight even when you're apart. At least from what I've been told."

I nearly choked on air as she seemed to confirm my earlier fear. "So, I'm going to be forced to be with him?"

That wasn't going to work for me. I would do whatever it took to prevent my life from being chosen for me. It didn't matter that Roman was delicious to look at. Or that his hands made my heart race like nothing before. Or how I noticed that the silver flecks in his eyes grew brighter when he stared at me.

Shit, I was in so much trouble.

"We don't think of it like that. It's all about perception. You can either see the bond as a gift or you can think of it negatively. Wolves live long lives, and being able to spend those decades with someone created just for you is rather appealing to most of us."

I listened to Embry speak, and there was a longing

in her words. I tried to understand where she was coming from, but that wasn't me. I might not be human anymore, but I wasn't a wolf. I still had very human and stubborn thoughts.

I wasn't born into this life. I shouldn't have even known it existed.

Except I did, and no matter how much I wished for a reset button, there was no going back to what I knew before.

Embry continued, "We're going to find out what all of this means. For now, you're in one of the safest places you could be, and you're the future mate to a fierce alpha. You've got nothing to worry about."

I laughed as I finished rinsing the conditioner from my hair. "Why isn't that comforting?"

She yanked the curtain back, scaring the hell out of me. "Because you've only been here a couple days. It will get easier to adjust as time goes by."

"And if I don't?" I asked, watching her face closely.

She shrugged. "I hadn't thought about that. Everything about you is new territory for most of us. Let's just hope I can convince you how badass being in the pack with me is, because I really am glad that you're here."

Embry walked out as I turned the water off. I was even more confused than when my head cleared after being around Roman. She mentioned the bond was a gift, which struck a chord with me while making my stomach churn.

Nothing was as simple as just accepting things as they came.

The mark, the bond, learning the things I always believed to be fiction were real… I needed to take it all in stride. As much as I wanted to run away because this was a lot, I was adult enough to understand the mark on my wrist wasn't going to go away on its own.

Sure, I could pass it off as a tattoo and move on, but there was more to my situation than that. There was an energy within it that not only I'd felt, but others, too.

For now, I was going to trust Embry was right and I was in the safest place I could be until we knew more.

When I exited the bathroom, Embry was humming in the kitchen and I headed to my room. The window was open. Heat from outside coated my skin like an unwelcome blanket. I shut the window and closed the blinds before getting dressed in another pair of jean shorts and a soft grey tee.

The knots were easy to pull from my hair after being washed, and I wrapped the strands into a loose bun on top of my head. Once I was ready, I went to the kitchen to find Embry making caramel brownies.

"Are you trying to bribe me?" I asked teasingly.

"Why ever would I be trying to do that?" she countered.

"Oh, I don't know. Maybe to sway me into staying here and not losing my damn mind."

She tapped her finger against her chin. "Possibly. Or maybe it's an apology. I know this isn't easy on you, and I don't mean to make light of your situation, but I hope you can see this as a blessing instead of a curse. I know it's not my life being directly affected, but I can't say I'm unhappy about anything that's happened. I'm a selfish bitch, and I won't apologize for it."

I took three steps and met her in the middle of the kitchen. Our arms wrapped around each other, and I held on tightly. With everything going on, I'd overlooked how exciting it was to meet Embry in person and not be having these conversations by video chat. *This* was a good thing, and I needed to be better at focusing on the positive things when they showed themselves.

We pulled apart, and I felt heaps better. "Thank you, Em."

"Don't thank me yet. I'm going to make you go to dinner with Roman still, but that's not until later. For now, we're going to wait for these brownies to be done and watch a chick flick. We can make fun of the mishaps in other people's lives while ignoring everything going on around here."

As much as I wanted to argue with going to dinner with Roman, I decided to have a human-type afternoon with my bestie instead. It had already been a hellish day, and some normalcy sounded like just what I needed.

11

CAIT

One thing was certain: I did *not* have a shifter metabolism. After two glasses, my reflexes slowed, and my skin tingled against the soft fabric of my shirt as I moved around on the couch. Embry enjoyed pointing out the flush in my cheeks as well.

"This is the most fun I've had in ages." She threw her head back and laughed as I giggle-snorted at nothing.

I was a hot mess but enjoying the hell out of it after the last few days.

"I hate to admit it considering you're laughing at my expense, but this really is great," I said with a sigh.

Embry choked from laughing so hard. "Oh, it gets even better."

My face heated as I checked myself over to make sure I didn't have anything on display that shouldn't be. "What?"

"Roman just reached out and wanted to know if you were ready for dinner," she said.

"Son of a bitch. I forgot about that." I hiccupped, covering my face. "I can't go to dinner with him. Tell him I'm sick and we can raincheck for… how about never?"

Embry shook her head at me and stayed quiet for a moment longer. As her silence stretched, my nerves shot up and I sobered some.

"What's going on?" I asked.

She held up a finger for me to be quiet, and I returned her gesture with one of my own. Another minute later, she smacked her hands together and grinned. "We're going to have a private group dinner."

"What does that mean?"

"It means instead of you being alone with Roman or showcased around the pack some more, we're going to head upstairs at the pack house to eat privately with Jack, Ramona, and Roman. Oh, and maybe Vaughn, too," she answered, getting up and going toward the stairs to her room.

"I'm in no condition to have dinner with the ruling pack family." From the sounds of how things worked around here, Jack and Ramona were like king and queen with Roman as the prince. Even though Roman was technically alpha, I hadn't missed how his dad commanded respect when I'd first shown up.

Embry ignored my question as she headed up the stairs to her loft bedroom. While I stayed put, I realized

I hadn't really asked anything at all. She simply chose to ignore my statement.

A few minutes later, she peeked back downstairs, and I still hadn't moved. Instead, I'd nearly fallen asleep as the alcohol-induced highs wore off.

"Get your ass off the couch. You're not getting out of this. I promise it will be fun," Embry said as a pillow hit me in the head.

"That was rude," I yelled back, only receiving a mutter in reply.

I got up and went to my room, wondering what the hell I was supposed to wear. I didn't know these people or what their expectations of me were. I'd met Ramona and she seemed nice enough, but maybe that was only curiosity. Had she known I was her son's mate when she came to see me? Maybe. She had ignored my question when I asked if I could have a mate.

Going to the mirror, I focused on brushing my hair out instead of finding clothes. Then, I decided a little makeup couldn't hurt to hide the dark circles that were starting to form under my hazel eyes.

Embry found me putting a few swipes of mascara on and I was instantly thankful I'd put the extra effort in. She was wearing a casual blue dress, and her hair was half-up with waves falling around her shoulders. My best friend was stunning.

"Why aren't you dressed?" she asked with a huff.

"Are we in a hurry?" I asked, tucking my makeup away before turning toward the closet.

She shrugged and sat on my bed as I considered

wearing black shorts and one of my nicer shirts. As I tugged on the sleeve of my favorite blue top, Embry nudged me out of the way. "Nope. First dinner, first impression. You need to look nice."

I raised a brow at her. "Are you saying my shirt isn't nice?"

"Oh, it is. For going to dinner with friends, but that's not what you're doing. It's not like this is a massive deal, but yeah. What about this instead?" She shoved a green dress with white swirl designs all over it at me. It was one of my favorites.

"Fine, but I'm not wearing heels. I don't trust myself after the drinks you gave me." I wasn't giggly anymore, but I wasn't sober either.

She grinned. "Good enough for me."

I quickly changed clothes and met Embry in the living room. She had a cheesecake in hand and was waiting by the door.

"Where'd that come from?" I asked about the dessert as she opened the door for me.

"My mama always taught me to bring a dish when invited to dinner. I keep a few things from the pack kitchen on hand. Sometimes I eat them on my own and sometimes I share," she answered as the door clicked shut behind us.

"Where are your parents?" I asked.

She glanced around, then lowered her voice. "They work for the supernatural council, but most people aren't supposed to know. They do a lot of undercover stuff, and I only see them a couple times a year. I promise to tell you more about it later."

I nodded, perfectly okay not knowing more for now. I had enough nerves about dinner. I didn't need to worry about supernatural spies existing in the world.

The alcohol was mostly out of my system by the time we arrived at the house. The large covered porch put off a welcoming vibe, which seemed odd for me considering wolves lived inside. The red front doors were something I'd always had on my bucket list for when I bought my own house.

Embry didn't stop to knock. She walked right in and waited for me to come inside. The entry was a mix of tans and whites with pops of colors that broke up the monotony. There was a sitting area that I could see and a half-circle wall with a cracked-open door. Just inside were bookshelves, and I wondered how big their library was.

Embry moved to the right and I followed her up a set of stairs. "Jack and Ramona live in the top story. Roman has the master room on the second floor, and there are two other bedrooms. One is used by Sam and the other is reserved for visitors. The lower level is offices, the kitchen, a game area, and food storage."

I smirked. I bet they had to keep a lot of food on hand, given they were literal animals.

"Who's Sam?" I asked.

"Roman's cousin." Before I could ask anymore, Ramona was smiling down at us from the top of the stairs.

"Hello, ladies. I'm so glad you could come," she said.

"I brought dessert." Embry held up the cheesecake as we got to the top.

Ramona winked, taking it from her. "Jack's favorite. Good call. He's been in a mood."

I tensed behind Embry, wondering if that mood had anything to do with me. I didn't want to be a problem for them. A large part of me wanted nothing more than to go back to not knowing about this part of the world. If my presence was causing issues or the mark was making others nervous, I'd have to be more careful.

"We'll figure it out. Cait will hopefully start showing signs of…well, anything, and maybe it will help," Embry offered.

Ramona waved her hand. "Cait doesn't need to do a thing." She looked around at me. "I don't want you to take our frustrations as a bad thing. We just want to help you and our son."

Ahh, so they knew about whatever this mate bond was. I wondered how many others knew.

Jack appeared over her shoulder. "You ladies going to stand out here and gossip, or come inside so I can have dessert first?" He plucked the cheesecake from Ramona's hands and kissed her on the cheek before disappearing back through their door.

For a brief moment, I'd forgotten Roman was there as we all headed in, laughing at Jack's antics. For just a second, I'd let my walls down, but as soon as we entered a small living room, my eyes landed on the imposing shifter.

Heat traveled through me, but I steeled myself and gritted my teeth. I would not let whatever juju he was putting off make me weak. I knew nothing about the man. It didn't matter that we were mates, especially since I didn't really know what that meant. I had things about myself to figure out first.

Roman smiled at me, and I was surprised by how much lighter brown his hair was when he wasn't covered in water.

Before things got awkward, I tore my gaze away from him and took in the rest of the area. There was a decent-sized kitchen with a double oven, a few closed doors, a ten-person dining table, and then the living room I was currently trying to avoid.

Embry tugged me toward the couch, and I kept my face neutral. "How's it going, Roman?" she asked as we sat down across from him.

I could feel his stare on me. I'd heard people say that before, but I always thought it was more of a metaphorical thing. No, this was very real, and my wrist began to pulse. Damn it, why was this so weird?

"Things are good, Embry. Though, they could have been better if my plans hadn't changed," Roman answered, and I could hear the smile in his words. Though, whether that was because there was an underlying threat in his words, or something else, I couldn't be sure.

I finally met his gaze and surprised even myself

when I was able to keep a straight face. Everything about him was intense, and I wouldn't lie to myself that there was an appeal—a strong one—but I wouldn't give in.

"Please tell me it's not going to be like this every time the two of you are around each other," Embry groaned.

I turned to her. "Like what?"

She tapped her nose. "I can smell the tension between you two. It's a bit much."

I gaped and tried to find the words to make it less embarrassing, but nothing came out as heat crept into my cheeks.

The pain of the mark hit new heights, and I hissed while shaking my arm out. Roman was at my side before I could take my next breath, followed by Embry. "What's wrong?" Roman asked.

"It's nothing new. Well, nothing new since it appeared. The mark burns sometimes," I answered.

"I thought you said it was more like pressure?" Embry asked.

By then, Jack and Ramona were there as well, and I was officially uncomfortable. "Well, it does that, too. That's the more common sensation."

"When does it get worse?" Jack asked.

Shit. I did not want to answer that.

I couldn't stop my eyes from meeting Roman's. Gone was the smirk he'd had on when I first arrived and in its place was only concern.

"Is it when you're around Roman?" Ramona asked,

and I nodded.

Jack made some weird noises and hurried off to one of the closed doors. He came back with a book as everyone except Roman gave me some room.

Jack kneeled before me and handed Roman the book. "Look at the middle section there, son."

While Roman read, Jack took my arm and pressed his palm over the mark. Relief was instantaneous, and I let out a sigh. "How did you do that?"

"Even though I'm not a reigning alpha, I will always hold some of the power since I was born with it. You hold untamed shifter magic within you, and it's drawn to my alpha power even though there is no wolf within you. I assume since Roman is an alpha and your mate, the draw is more severe and causing you discomfort."

Well, that made sense in a completely unrealistic way for my very human mind. A part of me was still hoping none of this was real, but with every new thing I learned, I was having a harder time ignoring the facts of my sudden reality.

"Do you think the new moon will force a shift on her?" Roman asked after he was done reading.

"It's hard to say. You of all people should be able to tell if she had a wolf. Since you can't sense one as alpha, then she might not be affected like the rest of us," Jack answered.

"What's that mean?" I asked. If I was going to be turning into a wild animal, I'd prefer to have a heads-up about it. You know, so I could schedule a massive breakdown into my week. Learning about wolves and becoming one were two completely different things.

"Wolves are at their strongest under a new moon. We don't have to shift, but the draw to do so is almost overwhelming. Our wolves have needs that we do our best to meet," Jack said as Roman kept scanning the pages of the book.

"We didn't invite Cait here to shove more information down her throat. Food is ready and it's time we got to know her a little better as a person instead of making her want to run away with all this wolf business," Ramona said as she shoved herself past her husband and son. "Come on. You can sit between me and Embry while we eat."

I smiled at Ramona, thankful for her interference. "I would love that."

Embry was at my other side and looped her arm through mine. "Have I told you lately how happy I am that you're here?"

"Yes, but you can keep saying it. Doesn't hurt my feelings any."

The two of them laughed, but I meant it. Remembering I'd come here because I trusted Embry was one of the only reasons that I hadn't run away screaming.

The thought of doing so was still appealing, but for now, I'd stay and hope that, sooner rather than later, someone could tell me what the hell being a Luna Marked meant.

12

ROMAN

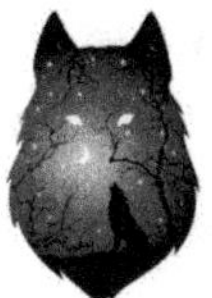

Dinner was painful to say the least. I'd invited Cait earlier so that we could spend time getting to know each other. I'd intended to cook spaghetti—the only meal I knew I wouldn't screw up—and take her to my cabin.

Sure, it might have been awkward at first, but I didn't see how we were supposed to get to know each other otherwise. Then, Embry stuck her tail where it didn't belong and I began to rethink my leniency toward her.

Embry got my mother involved.

Before I knew it, the dinner I'd planned was canceled and turned into a small gathering. One that, according to the others involved, would make Cait feel more comfortable.

Except that wasn't what happened. Instead, I'd learned that my presence made her feel worse rather than better. A fact that infuriated me to no end.

I sat opposite Cait at the table and watched her closer than was polite, but I'd also learned a significant amount.

When she was uncomfortable with a question, she tucked her hair behind her left ear. When she enjoyed a particular topic, her hazel eyes widened and sparked with intrigue while she gave whoever was speaking her full attention. Cait didn't do too much talking, but I was learning enough about her that I felt good about my next move.

She seemed to be more interested in listening and learning, so as dinner came to an end, I stood from my chair.

"Do you need help cleaning up, Mom?" I asked.

She shook her head. "I'm sure you have better things to do."

That I did.

Embry, you need to think of something to do. Now, I said through our wolf connection.

She's going to murder me in my sleep, but I love her and want her to be happy. Don't make me regret tricking her, Embry replied without looking my way.

"I'm going to head to the library tower. See if I can find any more books about the mark," I said and watched Cait.

Her brow arched and her breathing increased as I smelled her excitement, but she didn't look at me, even though I could tell my words intrigued her.

Dad started to say something, but Mom cut him off.

"Honey, I need your help. Can you start clearing the table?"

My mother winked at me, so I assumed she kept the conversation out loud to make it seem more normal for Cait. Dad grumbled but did as she asked.

Embry stood and groaned. "Damn. I was counting on Vaughn being here. I needed to go over some of the accounts for the mill with him. Cait, do you think you can find your way back to the cabin while I head to Vaughn's?"

Cait floundered for words. "Oh, um, I guess."

"I can take her," I offered immediately.

Embry clapped her hands, already standing. "Perfect." She leaned down and hugged Cait, who was the last one sitting. "I'll just be an hour or so."

Before Cait could object, Embry darted for the doors. *You owe me,* Embry added just for me.

As your alpha, I don't owe you anything, I replied.

You're right, but I also know you won't abuse that power. Just be good to Cait, she said before cutting off the connection.

Embry was right, but I didn't focus on her words for long, not when Cait seemed beyond nervous. She wiped her palms against her thighs, then pushed away from the table.

"You don't have to walk me back. I'm sure I'll be fine. It's not that far," she said, meeting my gaze and pushing her nerves down.

"What if I at least walked you to the door?" I asked,

hoping to show her that I wasn't trying to be overbearing.

She shrugged. "It's your house. I can't tell you what to do."

It took every effort not to smile. She was fighting getting to know me. I'd had a small hope that things might not be so difficult after our last meeting, but Cait seemed to have had a change of heart. I didn't exactly like it, but my wolf did.

If she wants to be chased, I have no problem doing so, he said.

Yeah, I didn't think you would. Just remember we need to be easy with her. She's not like us, I said.

Not yet anyway.

Unless my wolf knew something that I didn't, his use of the word "yet" was misplaced. So far, nothing had indicated Cait would shift, but it had only been a few days. When the new moon came in two weeks, maybe we'd know more.

Cait stood and began walking to the door when I didn't respond to her quip. I waved to my parents and ignored my mother's glowing face. She was a little *too* happy about me finding my mate, but I was proud of her for keeping her cool in front of Cait.

Cait was a quarter of the way down the stairs when I caught up to her. "Do you want a tour before you go?" I asked.

She flinched. "What?"

Something had her distracted, and I wanted to know what it was.

"Do you want a tour of the house?" I asked again.

"Embry sort of gave me one earlier," she replied.

Disappointment rolled through me. "So that's a no?"

Cait stopped at the second floor and sighed. "No, it's just... Never mind. If you really want to show me around, I won't object."

Irritation built deep inside me. I didn't like the mood she was in. I'd let myself believe that maybe this wouldn't be so bad, but Cait was proving nothing would be as simple as if she was a wolf. No matter my frustration with her change of demeanor, I wasn't going to give up trying to show her I was a worthy mate.

I wasn't sure what would happen if she rejected me and walked away from the pack. As far as I knew, no wolf had ever done that before to their mate. Sure, there had been bonded pairs that didn't get along perfectly, but they always found a way eventually.

"So, are we starting here?" Cait asked, glancing back at me, and I shook the thoughts from my head.

"No, these are just bedrooms," I said, assuming she'd have no interest in those. At least, not yet. Hopefully she would one day, if I did my job right.

If you can't figure out a way to get her interested, I'll be sure to pick up your slack, my wolf chided, and I ignored him. Cocky bastard.

Cait nodded, and the light from above caught her eyes. They seemed even brighter tonight, and I appreciated the dress she wore that complemented not only her eye color, but the curves of her body I was dying to explore.

Taking a chance, I rested my hand just above her waist and guided her down the remaining stairs.

She didn't flinch at my touch. Instead, she surprised me by relaxing, which had me doing the same.

Being alpha required me to maintain a certain stance around the pack. I wasn't overly friendly with the other wolves. I always alluded confidence and strength. My job was to be a person everyone could count on.

Being a younger alpha, that wasn't always an easy task, but I'd managed to do a decent job over the last few years with my dad's guidance. Now, I needed to find a balance between being a respectable alpha and a deserving mate, which was not as easy as I'd hoped.

We got to the first floor, and I went toward the kitchen and dining room. We had a commercial-sized kitchen and a dining room that was more like a mini cafeteria. There were two long wooden tables with bench seats that spanned twenty feet each.

"This is where those without family or anyone wanting to socialize eats. Pack members just need to give no less than one hour notice and the pack cooks prepare everything. Tonight is their night off, but this place is pretty crowded six nights a week," I said.

She tapped her fingers over the table without commenting and ventured through the arched doorway and into the kitchen where Vaughn was shoving the last of a sandwich down his throat. "Hey, guys."

"I take it Embry didn't find you," Cait huffed.

Vaughn glanced at me, but I let it go. Cait wasn't stupid.

"Uh, maybe I should go find her to..." Vaughn pleaded with me to give him something, but I just shrugged.

"It's okay, Vaughn. I'm starting to figure out what's going on," Cait said, but there was less bite in her words than I expected.

"Right. Well, I was out of mustard. I'm going to go now," Vaughn said, making a quick escape.

Cait turned to me as soon as we were alone and poked me in the chest. "I don't like the telepathy talk. If you want a moment alone with me, just ask. I don't like liars and don't appreciate you making my best friend lie."

"I'm sorry. It won't happen again," I replied sincerely.

"Did you want to tell me something?" she asked, tapping her foot and leaning toward me. I wondered if she was even aware of it.

I smiled down at her. "Not really, but you seemed interested in learning during dinner, so I was going to show you the library next and see what you thought."

Some of Cait's annoyance left her tense shoulders. "I guess that's fine with me."

I held my arm out. "Right this way then." We circled around the kitchen and exited through the other hallway. The bottom level of the house allowed for people to walk around in a circle, which saved us from backtracking when the offices were all in use.

We passed a couple of them before getting to the library tower. She went right through the door without waiting for me, then stopped just a few feet in to take in the room.

I would have given anything to hear her thoughts as she looked up at the fifteen-foot floor-to-ceiling bookshelves. There were two ladders on each wall with a spiral staircase in the far-right corner.

Cait's hand trailed over the shelves as the shock wore off. "How old are most of these books?"

"Decades to centuries. Most of them are wolf history-type books, but there are some classics and newer reads in here as well. By the window, there is a catalog to help you find whatever you might be looking for," I answered.

She nodded toward the stairs. "What's up there?"

"Go on up and see."

Cait glanced back at me, all earlier attitude replaced with mischief as she grinned. "Don't mind if I do."

My pulse picked up as I scented her excitement. If only I could tell whether the emotion was for me or the unknown of what she was going to find upstairs.

Definitely not you, but if you want to shift, I'm sure I can change that, my wolf said, and I chuckled.

I have no doubts, old friend.

13

CAIT

The mark on my wrist still pulsed as I followed Roman through the house, but there had been no more bursts of pain since before dinner. My hope was that the more I learned, the more control I could gain over the reactions I had. More likely, I was just getting used to Roman's presence, and I wasn't sure how I felt about that.

Either way, I was annoyed that Embry had set me up. I should have known something was going on when she darted off so quickly, but I hadn't suspected anything was amiss until it was too late.

Roman was being the perfect gentleman. I could tell my resistance to him was getting under his skin, but he didn't push for too much, and I was grateful.

I had wanted to check out the library since walking inside the house, so I didn't decline the invite, even when it meant spending more time alone with Roman.

The room was even more magnificent than I'd

imagined. The floor-to-ceiling mahogany shelves and rolling ladders had me itching to pretend I was Belle in the beast's castle. In a way, I guess I was. Except my beast was a wolf.

My beast.

Was he really mine, though?

Roman acted as if he wanted to be—at least he had throughout the day—but did *I* want him to be? Did I even have a choice? I needed to find out as soon as possible. Maybe somewhere in these books, I could learn more about wolf mates.

Except I had no desire to do that with Roman watching me.

With his encouragement, I headed up the stairs. They went straight up, winding tightly and giving my legs a workout I wasn't used to. When I got to the top, the area was open with a single table in the middle and a couch pushed against one of the two walls that were covered in more bookshelves.

While all of that was appealing, what caught my attention most were the windows on the outside wall. My feet moved without thought, and I pressed both hands against the glass as I took in the view. Once again, my previous misconceptions that Texas was a desert state were proven wrong. Everything I saw from the window was lush and full of life.

The sunset painted deep orange colors across the sky with flashes of red striking through it as the sun slowly descended behind the trees. Oregon had some amazing sunsets, but the serenity that settled deep into my bones was something else entirely.

"Beautiful, isn't it?" Roman whispered.

He was so close behind me that I could feel his breath on my neck as he said the words. My first reaction was to lean into him, but I stuffed that down and nodded. "I can see why Embry loves it here so much."

"My favorite place is on the roof of my cabin when the stars are out. There's nothing more peaceful," he said.

I took a step to the side to give myself some space before focusing back out the window. "Sounds like it."

A purple hue bled into the fiery sky, and I knew I could stand there all day watching the colors change. "Is this area open to everyone, or just certain people?" I asked, referencing toward the area behind us.

"You're welcome anywhere in this house, at any time," he replied.

I wanted to say something about not wanting to be just anywhere, but figured we really weren't at the joking stage of whatever this was between us.

"Thank you. I appreciate the hospitality," I said.

Roman reached for me, gently holding on to my hip. "Cait, I know—"

I cut him off. "Not now. I don't want to talk about the mark or mates or anything else wolf-related. Okay?"

He smiled, but I could tell it was forced. "Then, what would you like to talk about?" he asked.

Was there anything to say that didn't have to do

with wolf stuff? I had no idea. Part of me just wanted to be left alone, but I didn't want to be an asshole and ask him to leave what was technically his space.

When I didn't answer, he continued, "What did you do before going to Australia?"

This wasn't really any better as far as conversation went, but it was easier. I'd learned to say the words as if I was reading from a script. It helped to keep the emotions under wraps that I didn't like to share with strangers.

"My mom died, and, with Embry's encouragement, I went traveling. I spent a few years in foreign countries, doing whatever I wanted and seeing what I only dreamed of before. When I was ready to settle down but not come home, I found a job in Australia. I'd only been there a couple months when...well, you know."

I didn't look at Roman as I said the words. My gaze stayed on the vibrant patterns above the trees that were changing by the minute.

He kept his distance, but I could sense a rigidness set in. "I'm sorry you were alone dealing with a loss like that, but I can understand why."

I let out a slight chuckle. "Can you, though? Your parents are still alive and well." There was nothing I hated more than when others tried to compare grief. Not one person could understand another's, because even if it was the same kind of loss, the sorrow was never the same.

"My dad might be walking, but he nearly died a few

years ago and never fully recovered from his injuries. I shouldn't be the alpha so young, but he wasn't fit to face a challenger after he was attacked by a group of rogue wolves. When word got out, we knew it was only time before the other packs would come sniffing around.

"When they did, I was already alpha. We thought things would be okay, but the alpha of the west Texas territory is a ruthless bastard. He sent one of his own to challenge me. A move that was purely to break me, and it nearly worked. I was forced to kill a wolf who didn't deserve to die."

Shit, that was heavy. Much more than I expected to come out of him. His situation was nowhere near the same as mine but sounded just as painful. I couldn't imagine taking a life that wasn't deserving, and I found myself sympathizing with him.

He continued, "When I say I understand, I don't mean your situation, but about the need to get away. I wasn't in Australia for vacation. I was trying to get away for the anniversary of the day I killed that wolf. Some say my guilt is misplaced, the wolf would have killed me if I didn't end him first, but he was forced to challenge me. None of it was right."

"What kind of monster would send one of their own into a situation they knew the person couldn't survive?" I asked, not really expecting an answer. I was already aware the rules and structure of this world were completely different than anything I'd ever known.

Roman grunted, and his balled-up fist thudded against the window. "My grandfather."

My eyes widened. "What? Your grandfather wanted you killed?"

Roman laughed, but the sound contained no happiness. "No, but he wants our land, and he doesn't care at what price. He was trying to break me."

"Is this your mom or dad's father?" I asked.

"My mother's. She met my dad by accident. They were both in the right place at the right time you could say. Cohen, my mom's father, forbid her from ever seeing her mate again when he learned where my dad was from. You've met my mom, so you can imagine how well that went over. She left and never looked back. Fights have gone on over the decades because of it, but my parents wouldn't let anything come between them."

"Well, Cohen sounds like a grade-A dick. Have you ever met him?" I asked.

"A few times, but never like a grandson should meet his grandfather. But, none of that matters. He's nothing for you to worry about," Roman said, and hopefully he was right.

I turned away from the window, needing another distraction. Finding my way to the bookshelves, I traced my fingers over the spines and inhaled. The scent of old books filled my lungs, and I sighed. Anytime I visited a library, my favorite part was finding the oldest section in the building and literally smelling the history.

"You really like books, huh?" Roman asked.

I nodded. "It's been a while since I visited a library, and I don't read as often as I used to, but books will always be fascinating to me. The words paint a picture most minds could never imagine. They keep our ancestors alive. They help people escape. They bring hope when there is none."

"I mostly just thought they were to help people go to sleep," Roman said, and I jerked around intending to only glare at him. Instead, I accidentally elbowed him in the stomach and played it off as if I'd meant to.

"Don't disrespect books," I said before moving down the shelves.

There were only wolf-related books in this section. Most of the spines were titled East Pack and then a year ranging from 1803 until 2005.

"Do you guys not update the books anymore?" I asked, seeing as it's been more than a few years since the last one was created.

"We do, but the files are kept electronically now. Serene is our pack historian. She's transcribed most of these books onto computer files for us, so there isn't ever a chance of losing the history," Roman answered.

"Does she know anything about my mark?" I asked, even though I'd been the one to say we shouldn't talk about it.

"She knows a lot, but nothing that's been helpful so far. You're welcome to meet her whenever you're ready to ask any questions," he said.

"I'd like that."

After searching around the shelves for a bit longer,

the tension I held from keeping Roman at a distance was getting to me. Being around him was intense like nothing I'd ever known before. The pull my body felt toward him wasn't natural, but it was also a very real part of me that I couldn't ignore.

He watched me without judgment and let me do whatever I wanted, even when I knew he had plenty to say. The sense of rightness at being near him scared the hell out of me.

"I think I'm ready to head back to the cabin now," I said after peeking at a few of the generic wolf history books. Unfortunately, nothing had stood out to me that could be useful to my current situation.

Roman held his arm out toward the stairs. "Then, I'll walk you back."

I went down the stairs, having to watch my speed given how steep they were. When I got to the bottom, I stepped aside waiting for Roman to lead the way.

He surprised me by placing a hand on my mid-back and guiding me out the door. I thought once we exited the house, his hold would be removed. Instead, he kept me close and stayed by my side. It was an odd yet wholesome feeling. Roman didn't make me feel as if he was trying to put moves on me, but more so as if he was protecting me.

Though, I hoped there was nothing around here that I needed protecting from.

His head was constantly scanning the area as the sky darkened above us.

"Is there something I should be worried about?" I asked as I began to look around, too.

He shrugged. "It's just instinct. My wolf will never let his guard down when it comes to you, no matter where we are. The need to keep you safe is as strong as the need to breathe."

My chest tightened, and I sucked in air as I tried not to overreact to his words. It wasn't a line he'd forced out. He'd said them so naturally, as if I should have already known.

Unknown emotions ignited within my stomach as the cabin came into view. Suddenly, I wasn't ready for our night to be over, but I knew it was the right choice. It was hard for me to know if my reaction was real or something brought on by the mythical bond between us, and I needed to make sure nothing went too fast.

Roman stopped us about twenty feet from the front door. "Thank you for spending some time with me."

His left hand cradled my elbow, and a warmth traveled through my body, causing me to shudder. I didn't know what kind of magic he was packing, but it was powerful.

"Thanks for showing me the library," I replied.

The silver flecks glinted in his blue eyes as he peered down at me. My eyes went to his lips, and I had the urge to kiss them until neither of us could think straight. Before I could do something I'd probably regret, Roman tugged me into a hug, and his body heat enveloped me.

The sigh that escaped me couldn't be stopped as I

rested my head against his chest. Roman pulled back far enough to place a gentle kiss on my cheek that damn near reached the corner of my mouth before stepping several paces back.

"I'll see you soon, Cait," he whispered with a grin.

The comment stirred something inside me I tried hard to fight. It was sexy as sin, but also too self-pleasing. "Or maybe you won't," I replied, then spun around and stalked to the door.

Embry was waiting, likely having watched the whole thing, and let me in. I threw myself on the couch, my chest heaving with emotions and mind whirling with questions.

"What was all that about?" Embry asked.

"Your guess is as good as mine," I said, coming to the realization that fighting the attraction I had to Roman was going to be harder than I was prepared for.

14

CAIT

I'd spent the rest of the night trying to forget the interaction with Roman, but his touch seemed to be permanently branded into my memory. Watching a movie didn't help. Trying to read wasn't happening with my racing thoughts. Staring at the ceiling certainly hadn't done a damned thing, either.

Sexually frustrated had only been a term I'd used toward other people before, yet never really understood. Now, I did.

While there had been irritation swirling within me from Roman's grin, I couldn't forget the way I felt every time he touched me or the tender kiss he'd placed on my head. Everything about him was overwhelming. Okay, maybe not just him. The entire situation was overwhelming.

I was human, but I wasn't. I was marked by some wolf queen, but I wasn't a wolf. Nobody really knew what I was, and my frustration over that increased as I allowed myself to think about it more.

Having this bond thing with Roman was just the icing on the cake I wasn't sure I wanted.

Sure, I'd thought he was hot when we first met, so there was natural attraction, and he'd proven several times over that he could be respectful and caring, but the bullheaded part of me couldn't get over the fact that whatever Roman felt wasn't something that grew over time. The emotions were part of his DNA that told him he had to care for me as his mate.

I thought about Embry's previous words as the sun came up. My initial thought was that the bond was cruel for taking away a person's freewill, but to the wolves, it was a gift. They lived long lives, and having a partner meant just for you to spend those years with was sacred.

I saw her point, and it made sense, but my still-human mind couldn't see past the fact that my choices were being taken away. I'd had no option to deny the mark. No option to choose if I wanted to be bonded. No option to be me.

Now I was stuck with an attraction I was fighting and a mark that held power nobody really understood.

Time was up in the feeling-sorry-for-myself department, though. I needed to find answers. I needed to get a better understanding of whatever situation I'd found myself in. I thought about asking Embry to take me to Serene, the historian Roman had mentioned, but instead, I was going to get dressed and head to the pack library.

People seemed to come and go through the house, so I hoped I could sneak in and get some reading done without being seen. As I got dressed and had a new sense of determination, I opened my door to find Embry already awake and sitting at the computer by the kitchen.

"Good morning," I said, heading to the kitchen for some tea.

"Did you sleep okay?" she asked.

I shrugged. "What are you working on?"

"Accounting stuff for the mill. I need to head there today. Do you want to come with me?"

I already had plans, but the thought of seeing the more human side of the wolves was too good to pass up. "What time?"

"I'll be working on these reports for a couple more hours and then we could go. Vaughn said he'd entertain you until then if you were bored," Embry said.

"Yeah, I'll go with you. I don't need a babysitter, though. Unless it's not safe for me to be alone." I remembered the way Roman had been on guard last night, and my wrist warmed as his words rang through my mind… *The need to keep you safe is as strong as the need to breathe.*

Damn it, I was trying to avoid those thoughts.

"You're fine to go out on your own; just stay away from the forest. Not because anything will get you, but because it's easy to get lost. Until you know your way around better, just stick to the main trails and areas." Embry turned back to her computer, her fingers flying over the keyboard. I finished making my tea while she worked.

When I was done, I stopped at the front door. "I'll be back in a couple hours."

"You're actually leaving?" Embry's eyes widened as she paused work.

"I need to face the facts sooner rather than later, don't I?"

She grinned. "That's my girl. If you need anything, you know where to find me. Roman will be around as well."

I nodded and opened the door before saying goodbye. I didn't intend on needing anyone. I knew where the library was, and it seemed easy enough to navigate.

The walk to the main house was tense as I watched my surroundings. I couldn't even be sure what day of the week it was, because I hadn't been checking my phone, but there was much less commotion around the pack than there had been the couple of days before.

As I entered the house, I heard Ramona's voice down the hallway. I wasn't sure who she was talking to, but the sounds drew closer, so I darted into the library, leaving the door cracked behind me.

Turning around, I scanned the room and breathed a sigh of relief when I found no one else in the room. Given I'd found a lot of wolf books upstairs, it was the first place I wanted to look. Going up the steep stairs made my legs ache even more the second time around and reminded me I wasn't one who did lots of exercise.

I let out a groan when I made it to the top and went straight for the table in the middle. There were new books out, and I searched the room, but still found myself alone. Being nosy, I peeked at what the previous person was reading and found strips of paper sticking out the edges.

Opening to the first page, there was a note that only read *human* followed by two question marks with three hard lines struck beneath the word. I flinched at the aggressiveness and assumed it had everything to do with me.

I peeled the paper up and read the two pages. They spoke of mates bonding for life. There was brief mention of rejected mates and the effects it had on the inner wolf. My chest ached as I read those words, and I hated the guilt I felt at wondering if I was hurting Roman's wolf.

On the next page, there was a mention of the possibility that wolves could bond with other supernaturals like witches, vampires, and fae, then references to another section for further detail. I flipped to another marker, this one containing more notes.

The mark contains power descended directly from the moon goddess. Those who harness the gift are worthy of any mate they choose.

I had a choice? Well, that was new information and something that brought my irritation levels back up.

The metal stairs creaked as someone came up. I shut

the book, slid it away from me, and turned for the shelf behind me.

A groan sounded from behind me, and I caught sight of an older woman holding way too many books.

Running toward her, I grabbed as many as I could. "Let me help."

"Thank you, dear," the woman muttered as her face came into view, no longer covered by the stack of books.

She had wrinkles around her soulful brown eyes, and straight grey hair that ended just past her shoulders. "You must be Cait. I'm Serene," she said politely once all the books were on the table.

Ah, I should have known. "It's nice to meet you, Serene. I was hoping to at some point, but thought I'd start with the library first."

She smiled at me, the lines around her eyes deepening. "Smart girl. Better to come with answers than questions."

Well, that made absolutely no sense, but I let the comment go as she started to file the books she'd brought up. She hummed as she flitted about the room, and I grabbed one of the wolf mate books. I wanted to know more about the comment I'd read about possibly choosing my own mate.

Serene tsked at me as I sat. "You won't find what you want in there."

"Then, where might I find it?" I asked.

"Well, if I knew that, then you wouldn't be looking, would you?" She laughed, and I sighed.

Maybe the pack historian wasn't going to be as helpful as I'd hoped.

A few minutes later, she tossed a few books at me and took one from the pile on the table. "The men around here are stubborn, but they mean well. Jack and Roman have been working around the clock to find out anything that can explain how you got that mark." She nodded toward my wrist. "But they won't find the answers they seek within the books."

"Then, why did you give me more books?" I asked.

"Because you just might. At least enough to help you figure out the rest on your own. Just be careful. Some of those passages are easy to mistranslate." She flipped open the book I'd first been looking at and straight to the note I'd last read. "Take this for instance. No wolf can choose their true mate, but a Luna Marked can choose *a* mate if they decide it's the best choice. Do you understand?"

"I don't have to accept my true mate, and I could still find another wolf to bond with, but it wouldn't be the same as a true mate," I said.

She patted my hand. "You're smarter than most humans. Makes sense why you're not one."

This woman was batty as hell, but she was quickly growing on me.

"Just remember, Roman is indeed your true mate. You share a bond with him that was formed the moment that mark appeared on your wrist, but you are not mated. All wolves have to accept their partners, and until you can fully accept what you are, Roman is just a man you'd like to hump," she said, and I nearly choked on my own air.

"I can't believe you just said that." I began to laugh as I leaned back in the chair.

"I've lived for over three hundred years. Keeping my thoughts to myself isn't as fun as saying whatever comes to mind," she said.

"Well, I hope I can be you when I grow up, then."

She reached for me once more, this time holding on to my hand. "No, dear. You're going to be so much more once you figure out what you're capable of."

I raised a brow at her. "If I asked, would you explain that more?"

"I told you. It's better to come to me with answers and not questions. I'll tell you more when you can tell me more."

"Yeah, I'll get right on that," I muttered, and she got up.

"You're going to be okay, Cait. Just focus on who you are and what you feel on the inside. Everything else on the outside is just noise for now."

That was the first thing she'd said that I could use. "Thank you."

She nodded and headed back down the stairs with her back straight and head high. For a centuries-old woman, she was in good shape.

I took her advice to heart and stacked the books I was interested in together, hoping that there wouldn't be an issue with me taking them from the library. When

I made my way back downstairs, the door was open, and I heard loud voices in the entryway.

Setting the books down, I hurried to see what was happening, and my blood turned to hot rage.

A petite young woman with a white-blonde pixie cut, short black shorts and a thin white tank top had her body wrapped around Roman, and he was grinning from ear-to-ear.

"I've missed you so much," he said as he held her tight.

"What the fuck?" I snarled, and Roman immediately dropped her, but it was too late. I'd already seen enough.

15

ROMAN

It had been nearly five weeks since I'd last seen Sam. We were cousins, but she was also my best friend. Her parents died when she was thirteen, and my parents raised her through the teen years. It wasn't always easy living with her, but I wouldn't have traded her for anything.

She was supposed to have been back the same day I was, and I could have really used her throughout all the craziness of finding Cait, but I knew her job wasn't always predictable. She didn't work for the supernatural council, but she was contracted by those who did.

When Sam went on missions, she wasn't allowed to bring a phone or make any contact home. We often went weeks without knowing if she was alive or dead, but given what I knew she was capable of, I tried to keep faith while she was away that nothing could best her.

Sam waltzed through the door as I saw Serene leaving. I'd tried to catch the historian to see if she would meet with Cait, but seeing Sam had taken precedence.

"Welcome home, Sammy," I said as she yelled and jumped into my arms.

I was the only person in the world Sam showed affection to and the only one allowed to call her anything but Sam. Her given name was Samantha, but after losing her parents, she never again went by it and put all her efforts into becoming a warrior.

"Sorry I was late, Ro," she said.

"I've missed you so much," I replied and began to tell her we had a lot to catch up on, but my blood went cold before I could.

"What the fuck?" Cait said before storming out of the house and slamming the door so hard behind her that the windows rattled.

Sam pulled her head back and let go of me. "Who was that?"

"My mate," I answered.

Sam punched me in the ribs. "Seriously, dude? Why didn't you tell me?"

I groaned. "You just got here. When was I supposed to tell you?"

I moved to the door, intent on catching Cait, but Sam stopped me. "Tell me how this happened."

"She doesn't know who you are, and that probably didn't look the way it should have to her."

"You've got to be shitting me." She sighed and I

didn't want to hurt her feelings, but Cait needed me more. Actually, *I* needed Cait to hear me out more.

Sam rolled her eyes. "What are you still doing here? Go get her, idiot, and then come back and tell me how the hell this happened."

I didn't bother to respond before I darted out the door. My wolf pushed to the surface, and we scented the air for the direction she might have gone.

North, my wolf said, and I raced forward.

Cait didn't have wolf speed, so I wasn't worried about losing her, but I was concerned with how things would play out. The good thing was that her anger showed she actually had feelings for me. If she didn't give a shit about me, she wouldn't have stormed out.

Don't be so full of yourself. Cait isn't going to be easy to tame, my wolf said.

Now *you say that? What happened to all that confidence you were spewing a couple days ago?*

We've had time to get to know her a little better. I've spent that time listening, and confidence isn't going to win her over.

No shit, I thought.

Finally, she came into view and I cut off the conversation. "Cait, hold up a minute," I called out.

She flipped me off and kept walking. I couldn't help the grin that appeared. Angry Cait was adorable and attractive.

I reached for her hand, but as soon as my fingers brushed against hers, she whirled around at me. "No. You don't have permission to touch me."

I jerked my arm back and felt like she kicked me in the balls. She was more than mad, and I didn't know what to do.

"Cait, that was—"

"I don't need to hear about your hookups. We're not together. Not now, not ever. You don't need to feel obligated to me just because some freaky magic says so. Go back to her and live your life." She turned back toward the forest, eager to get away from me.

Nope. I wasn't letting this happen.

"Damn it, Cait." I grabbed her waist and threw her over my shoulder. "You're going to listen to me whether you want to or not."

"Embry!" Cait screeched as I tightened my hold.

Embry, if you come to her right now, your rank in this pack will be severely impacted, I threatened through our wolf link.

You're an asshole, was her only reply, but it was good enough for me.

"Embry isn't coming. Quit screaming," I said as I headed toward my cabin since we were already in that direction.

Cait didn't listen and kept calling for Embry while pounding her fist into my spine. For a human, she was stronger than I expected, but that was probably only adrenaline. My arms stayed locked on her legs so she couldn't kick me in the balls. Then, I ran.

Within a minute, she was out of breath and we had made it to the cabin. I didn't let her down until I kicked the door closed behind me and tossed her on the bed.

"That was Sam. My cousin. She has been gone for over a month. She is also my best friend, and that was *not* what it looked like," I said with more authority in my voice than I intended.

Cait shrank back for only a second as my alpha power tried to settle over her. She hissed and snarled at me. "You had no right to bring me here."

"I had every right. You were trying to leave for a reason that didn't exist," I snapped.

She stood on the bed and was a few inches taller than me. That seemed to give her a confidence I hadn't seen since I first met her. "I don't need a reason to want to leave. Maybe I'm just done being here."

"We're not even close to being done, darlin'." She was making me so angry, my southern drawl was coming out.

I saw a flash of something unfamiliar in her eyes right before she pushed against my chest. I ended up ten feet in the opposite direction, smacking my head against a chair.

"Oh, my God." Cait was still standing on the bed, her hands covering her mouth and eyes wide.

"Seems to me you've channeled some of that power we've been feeling from the mark," I said as I got up, "but that is something to discuss later. I need to know you believe me and that you're not leaving."

Cait was in shock, and I didn't want to pressure her, but I needed her word that she wouldn't just take off, especially not after what she'd just done.

"I believe you," she said, but it was muttered from between her fingers still covering her face.

I went to her, moving her arms down slowly. "Cait, it's okay. You didn't hurt me."

"What did I do?" she asked.

"You defended yourself, as you should have."

Some of the shock finally wore off. "Well, you shouldn't have taken me like a psycho."

She had a point.

My wolf stirred. He wanted out. He wanted to claim her as our own more than any other time we'd been with her. The thought of Cait leaving us drew a panic in him I'd never known.

"I'm sorry," I said as I tried to make the situation better.

"I guess I'm sorry, too. I don't know why I reacted like that."

I grinned, unable to help myself. "Because you like me."

She glared at me. "No, I don't."

"Your denial will just make it that much sweeter when you finally admit it." I was unsure why I was taunting her, but it felt right.

"Take me back," she demanded, her hazel eyes growing darker around the edges.

I tightened my hands around her hips. "What if I don't want to?"

Cait sucked in a breath but didn't drop the tight look in her eyes. "Don't make me ask twice."

"You haven't even asked once, but I'm curious. What do you plan to do if I don't?"

She poked her finger in my chest. "I'm not sure, but we can find out if you insist on doing this the hard way."

Ha. She was threatening me. That was something new, and I liked it.

"Alright, Kitten. We'll do it your way. Today. Would you like to walk back, or would you like me to run with you?" I asked.

She sneered when I called her Kitten, but I couldn't help it. She was feisty yet irresistible, just like one.

Cait crossed her arms. "I'll walk by myself. Just point me in the right direction."

"Yeah, that's not going to work for me and my wolf." I picked her up again, this time cradling her against my chest instead of tossing her over my shoulder as we walked out the door. She punched me in the shoulder and, when that didn't work, I caught a right hook in the jaw.

"You can't just keep kidnapping me," she said when it didn't appear as if her super strength was going to come back.

"I'm not this time. I'm returning you. Safely."

You shouldn't be returning her at all. We could just keep her at the cabin, my wolf said, and I smirked.

"What's so funny?" she asked as I began to slow. We were close to the house, but I didn't want to leave her without making sure she wasn't upset with me.

"My wolf wants to keep you locked in the cabin," I answered honestly.

"Well, your wolf is even more psycho than you are," she said.

"Possibly, but it's only because he cares so much. You don't know what it means for him to find a mate."

Some of the tension left her body then, and I set her down.

"I'm sorry for taking you, but at least it wasn't wasted. We proved you can access the power within you."

That comment didn't seem to make her feel better. In fact, she stepped further away from me.

"Hey, there's nothing wrong with what you did. We just need to figure out how to trigger it without making you upset," I said.

She laughed. "I think you rather enjoyed that part."

"Maybe parts of it," I admitted.

"How about you introduce me to Sam, and I'll worry about the rest later?" she suggested, and I had no problem with that.

"It would be my pleasure."

Placing my hand on her back, I guided her into the house and hoped like hell Sam was on her best behavior. I didn't want to regret the two of them meeting.

16

CAIT

I hadn't gotten a good look at Sam when she'd been wrapped around Roman, but what I had seen was stunning. The fury I'd felt at what I thought was Roman's betrayal surprised the hell out of me, but a part of me was glad it happened.

None of it had felt forced. The feelings had belonged to me, and a sense of control had settled within me when so many things had seemed out of my hands. The only thing I could have done without was the sudden burst of strength I'd had when I let Roman get really under my skin.

That had scared the shit out of me but was also intriguing.

Sure, learning about wolf shifters was a lot. Being told I was marked by their creator was even more overwhelming, but wielding the power the others kept talking about? That was a whole different thing.

One I was determined to learn more about. Right after I met Sam.

She was sitting at the base of the stairs, her long legs stretched out as she leaned back without a care in the world. Her skin was light, as if she hated the sun. Her short hair was an unnatural white-blonde, and her eyes were a bright blue that screamed trouble.

When she stood, I realized she wasn't all that tall—maybe a few inches over five feet—but she held herself like she was the biggest person in the room.

"I'm Sam McIntyre. You can call me Sam or Mac, but never anything else unless you want to be punched in the vagina." She held out her hand to me, and I smirked. Wolves had an odd way of introducing themselves, but I appreciated the bluntness.

"Nice to meet you, Sam. I'm Cait Jones, and I only go by Cait," I replied, holding her stare. Somehow, I could sense she was sizing me up, and I wasn't going to let her think I was weak.

"Fair enough. How did you meet my cousin?" she asked, taking a step back when Roman leered at her.

"He found me on the beach and acted like a wet dog. I thought I'd lost him but ended up here by pure coincidence. Embry is my best friend."

Her eyes widened. "You're *that* Cait? Well, shit. I can't believe I missed all of this."

"Did you get the job done?" Roman asked her.

She grunted. "Would I be here if I didn't?"

"Probably not. Now, are you done with your questions? I'm sure Cait wants to go back to Embry's."

Sam's eyes went up and down my body twice before settling back on my face. "I like her. For now. Maybe we'll get to know each other better later. I have another job, and I'll be leaving again within the next couple of days." She spoke to Roman but continued to stare at me.

I didn't let her 'for now' statement bother me. I knew her type. She wanted a reaction, and I wasn't going to give her one.

I smiled sweetly at her. "I look forward to when you return."

Sam chuckled and walked off without making a noise. She was light on her feet, and I wondered what kind of skills she had that signed her up for secret missions or whatever it was she'd been doing.

Roman reached for me when we were alone. His eyes said he had a lot to say, but I'd reached my limit for the day. I was ready for a break, and Ramona arrived just in time to give me one.

"Ro, dear. Can you come help—" She cut her sentence off when she saw me. "Oh, I didn't realize you were busy."

"Roman was just returning me after kidnapping me. He's not busy now." I moved out from under his hand that rested on my shoulder and dashed out the door.

I heard a thud followed by low, hissing voices, but I didn't bother to turn around. Freedom was more important than anything else in the moment.

Within minutes, I was back at Embry's and hoped I hadn't missed her before she took off to the mill. I was curious about what went on there and how they interacted with the public.

She was just coming downstairs as I walked in the door. "Oh, good. You're back. I was afraid I was going to have to leave you behind. Vaughn is over there already, since you didn't need a babysitter, and keeps texting me to hurry up. Let's go."

Embry grabbed on to my hand, and we speed-walked to a detached garage on the other side of the pack house. She punched a code into the door and grabbed keys off the wall when we entered.

"We're taking the jeep. Hop in," she said.

I got into the passenger seat of the topless black Wrangler as she opened the garage door and started up the jeep. It wasn't until we were headed down the paved driveway that she spoke. "So, are you going to tell me how your outing was, or do I have to force it out of you? Also, you should bring your phone with you in case you get lost."

Laughter bubbled in my chest as the wind twisted my hair around my face. I gathered it to one side and glanced her way. "Well, I went to the library in the pack house. I found some interesting books. I met Serene—someone who is either the most awesome old lady ever or batshit crazy. Then, I was kidnapped."

Embry grinned. "I was wondering if you'd mention that."

"You knew?" Oh, I was going to kill her.

"Well, I didn't have advanced notice. I heard your shouts and was going to go check on you, but Roman said I wasn't allowed to save you or my standing within the pack would be impacted. I called him an asshole if that helps."

It didn't really, but I understood why she hadn't interfered.

"Well, it wasn't a total loss. I zapped the hell out of him by accident."

Embry tapped the brakes, but someone was behind us, so she had to keep going. "Okay, you totally should have led with that. What do you mean by 'zapped'?"

I shrugged. "Well, it didn't feel like a zap to him, but it did to me. He pissed me off, and I sent him flying across the room with a shove I wouldn't have been capable of before."

"Interesting. Did you only do it once?" she asked.

I grimaced. "Unfortunately."

"Oh, man. This is almost too much fun."

"I don't see anything fun about this situation," I said.

"You will. At some point. What's important is you accessed power from the mark. We weren't sure if you'd be capable of doing anything like that. Now, we can work on drawing it out and figuring out how you control it."

While I'd been curious about the power I held earlier, I wasn't so sure now that Embry was planning on "drawing it out". What if I couldn't control it? The fact that there wasn't much to go on when it came to the mark didn't leave me super optimistic about trying again now that I'd had some time to think about it.

"I promise nothing bad will come of it. We might not know everything, but I know enough that I wouldn't ask you to try if I thought you were at risk of being hurt. If anything, I'm the one in danger." She grinned, but I didn't find her statement entertaining.

I considered her words, and she quieted as we drove the few miles to the mill. When we arrived, she turned down a dirt road that led back to big warehouses and large machines I knew nothing about. There were various types of wood stacked everywhere and forklifts moving things around.

She parked the jeep in front of the first building. "This is the customer area. They're not allowed anywhere else on the property except here and the parking lot." She pointed to a chain-link gate. "If there are big orders, trucks back up there and we bring things around."

"I guess privacy would be a big deal for you guys," I said.

"No. It's more about insurance. We don't need some idiot getting squished by a log because he doesn't know what he's doing."

That made sense, too.

We entered the building, and it reminded me of a hardware store. There were several rows of smaller, miscellaneous items and a wide counter toward the back wall.

A young girl waved. "Hey, Embry."

"Hi, Chloe. This is Cait. She's staying with me at the property."

I noticed Embry hadn't said pack, and I wondered if they'd trained themselves not to use certain words outside of their land.

"Oh," was all the girl said before she busied herself with paperwork I wasn't convinced actually needed attention.

Embry didn't say anything and took me around to the back. "This is my work office. I share it with Vaughn. I'm sure you can understand why I prefer the desk at my house."

Rumbling laughter sounded from behind us. "You know you're secretly in love with me."

Embry gagged as Vaughn entered the room from another door at the back. "Only in your dreams, big guy."

He waggled his eyebrows and grinned wide. "Emphasis on the big."

I couldn't stop my smile from growing even if I wanted to. I wondered if maybe Embry did have a crush on Vaughn. They were a lot alike. She was possibly too stubborn to admit it, though.

"I finished the reports at home. What did you need to show me here that had you annoying me for the last hour?" Embry asked him.

He pulled paint samples from his back pocket. "Our office is getting an upgrade. Which color do you like least?"

She sighed. "You've got to be shitting me. You couldn't have just asked me when you got back?"

"Clearly you know nothing about design." Vaughn

walked over to the wall and spread the paint samples out. "You have to see them in the room to make the right decision."

Considering Vaughn was way into his motorcycle and sported a leather jacket that screamed bad boy, I wanted to say I was surprised by this side of him, but in some weird way, it made sense.

I pointed to the soft yellow. "That one might make the two of you want to kill each other less."

Vaughn nodded. "Sexual frustration is a bitch. You might be onto something, Cait."

Embry threw her hands in the air and headed for the door. "I'm never working in this office again."

"Do you want to help me?" Vaughn asked.

"I don't actually think you need help," I replied.

He smirked. "Yeah, you're right. I just wanted to annoy her."

"Job well done. Now, I'm going to go find her before she leaves me behind."

I turned for the door, but Vaughn grabbed my hand. "How is everything with Roman?"

I did not want to talk about this with Vaughn of all people.

"Everything is fine," I said while taking a step closer to the door.

He sighed. "I don't like to get involved in other people's business," he said, and I tilted my head to the side with feigned shock. "Okay, maybe I do, but Roman isn't just my alpha. He's also one of my closest friends. If he does something stupid, all I ask is that you try to give him some grace. The two of you were raised in different worlds, and there's bound to be some bumps in the road."

Vaughn released me, and I nodded. "I appreciate the advice. I'm doing my best to keep an open mind. You might want to tell him it's not polite to kidnap people, though."

Vaughn's bellowing laughter followed me as I headed back into the main part of the building. Embry was nowhere in sight, and neither was the girl who'd been at the counter. I went to the door and saw Embry waiting in the jeep.

After climbing in, I turned to her. "So, you and Vaughn?"

She groaned. "He's been getting under my skin since I started working at the mill, but it's all in fun. We've never hooked up, and I don't plan on changing that fact. Ever."

Her comment got me thinking. She'd never talked about boyfriends before, and I hadn't had one since I'd known her unless I counted the guy from France who followed me around for a bit.

"Do wolves sleep around like humans? Can you get diseases?" I asked. Okay, I wasn't really concerned with STDs. The conversation made me wonder about Roman's past, and I tried to ignore the growing jealousy caused by thoughts of him with other women.

"Supernaturals don't get sick. Like ever, and that includes nasty human diseases." Embry shuddered. "As for sleeping around, some of us do and some don't.

We don't think of sex and virginity like humans do. It's more of a natural thing and nothing to be ashamed of."

Well, that didn't really answer my unasked question, but it wasn't something I really needed to worry about until I decided how exactly I wanted to move forward with things.

Roman very clearly wanted me to consider being mates with him, but he was going to have to deal with the fact that I still considered myself human and needed more time.

"What about you? You've always been so quiet about the topic, and given I had a pretty big secret of my own, I never pried," Embry said.

"Oh, well, there have been two guys, but one was a long time ago, and the other was Francis, the guy I told you about while I was abroad."

She hummed. "Yes, the yummy French. Gods, his accent was delicious."

She wasn't wrong about that, but he'd been too clingy, and I'd finally cut things off after a few months.

We got back to the pack and parked the jeep. When we came out of the garage, I heard loud noises and turned around. Chunks of wood thudded to the ground, and I moved closer.

Roman was shirtless with his back to us, chopping logs. Why he was doing that when it was hot as hell outside, I didn't know, but I forgot every reason why I didn't want anything to do with him.

His muscles rippled as he lifted the axe up and slammed it down into another piece of wood. There was a large tattoo covering nearly his whole back that I hadn't seen before. It was a twisted tree, bare of any leaves, and there were layers of depth to the drawing. The finer details, I couldn't see, and I couldn't deny I didn't want to.

Embry nudged me. "You've got a little drool on your chin."

Roman froze mid-strike, and I backed up quickly. Given how much I didn't want to accept fate choosing the person I was supposed to love, I didn't want to give Roman the wrong idea by staring. He seemed to have enough confidence without my help.

"You're an asshole," I muttered, hoping Roman hadn't seen me running off.

She caught up and swung her arm around my shoulders. "No, I'm just telling it like it is. You can fight this all you want, but I know you and I know what I'm seeing. Things will work. I'm sure of it."

Unfortunately, I didn't believe she was right—for several reasons, but one that was most obvious. I might not be quite human anymore, but I also wasn't a wolf.

The sooner people stopped trying to pretend otherwise, the better off we'd all be.

17

CAIT

I hadn't eaten yet, so we made sandwiches at Embry's house. She didn't say anything else about Roman, and I was thankful. I just wanted the subject to be left alone. Things were hard enough as it was. I knew a part of me was merely being obstinate—I'd been that way my whole life—but I needed to focus on one thing at a time. Whatever was inside me seemed most pertinent.

"So, you mentioned something about training?" I asked Embry when we were done with food.

"You want to start today?"

I nodded. "No time like the present."

"Alright, then. Go change into some workout clothes, and we'll head out to the fields," she said.

"Uhh, can I borrow some workout clothes?" I'd only set foot in a gym once. I made it a whole five minutes before I'd hightailed it out of there and never turned back.

She shook her head at me. "Just wear pajama shorts and a tank top. We won't be doing anything crazy."

Thank God for that.

I quickly changed and met her by the door. She was wearing yoga pants, a tight tank top, and had her rose-gold hair styled in a messy ponytail. Basically, she looked like a model, and I was her frumpy friend in baggy black shorts and a plain white tee. Good thing I didn't really care what anyone here thought of me.

"Ready?" she asked with a wide smile.

"No and yes," I answered honestly.

She looped her arm through mine as we made our way out the door. "Don't worry, friend. I promise not to do anything too crazy. This is new for all of us."

"Should we have supervision?" I asked. While I trusted Embry, she wasn't old and excelled in accounting and investments. This seemed a bit out of her expertise.

"Depends on how things go. If you start showing signs of crazy strength and power, then probably. For now, we'll see. I'm worried if you have too many people around, you won't relax and it won't work."

She wasn't wrong about that.

We arrived at a grassy area about five minutes past Vaughn's house. It was quiet and peaceful, surrounded by trees. The sun was beating down on us, and I was already sweating just from the walk over, but I wasn't uncomfortable from the heat.

"So, tell me exactly what happened when you shoved Roman," Embry said.

"Roman was in my face, and he wouldn't back away. I was beyond frustrated and pushed him. Right before I did, I felt a surge of energy within my body and somehow channeled it through my hands. He pissed me off again, but I couldn't find the source of whatever I'd tapped into the second time."

"I take it you don't feel it now, then?" she asked, and I shook my head. "Well, let's try meditating first."

"And if that doesn't work?" I asked.

She smirked. "Then, I'll try pissing you off."

Something told me she would enjoy that a hell of a lot more than I would.

Embry directed me to the grass where we sat cross-legged next to each other. I'd never even done yoga, so I was already uncomfortable but tried to roll with it.

"Relax your muscles. Keep your back straight and chin slightly down. You'll want to breathe in through your nose and out through the mouth as you gaze out into the trees. Don't try to focus on any one thing, though. Once you feel your body loosening, close your eyes," Embry said in a soft voice.

This was awkward and harder than I thought it would be. My mom used to be obsessed with pregnancy shows, so I tried to recall the breathing exercises I'd seen a million times before. It seemed like the same concept, because it was all about calming the body.

"As soon as you're ready, you'll want to scan your body with your eyes closed. Visualize yourself internally and search for what you seek. If there are blocks in your way, don't avoid them. Clear them up," Embry added, and I was starting to think I had no idea who she was.

Regardless, I did as she asked, but couldn't sense any blocks. Instead, the motions further relaxed me, and I zoned out as my breathing evened. After a few minutes, there was a pulsing at my wrist. My first thought was to open my eyes, but instead, I did another scan on myself.

Finding nothing, I tried again and again. Embry stayed quiet, so I assumed I was doing something right, or maybe she'd fallen asleep. Either way, there was a change happening. I just had to grab hold of it.

The pounding increased and moved into my core. My eyes either imagined it as a purple light or I was actually seeing whatever was inside me. I visualized the power moving from my center and expanding into my arms and legs.

The energy trickled slowly through me, and a pureness I'd never known settled over my body. There was strength and peace and certainty all wrapped into one.

"Holy shit," Embry muttered, her worry breaking through my concentration.

My eyes opened, and I lost hold of the power. "What happened?"

"You were glowing purple. Not super bright, but there was a soft hue around you that was putting off some serious heat," Embry answered.

At least I hadn't been imagining the color I was latching on to.

"Is that a bad thing?" I asked.

She shrugged. "It's not a normal wolf thing, but you're not a normal wolf."

"No, she isn't," another voice said from behind us.

I turned around to see Serene walking up with Ramona. Serene wore loose cotton clothing and had her greying hair wrapped in a tight bun.

"What are you two doing out here by yourselves?" Serene asked.

"I didn't know we needed a babysitter," Embry replied confidently.

"You do when you're messing with things you don't understand. Cait can't hurt herself, but it doesn't mean she won't hurt you," Serene said.

"What do you mean I can't hurt myself?" I asked.

"Your power won't attack its host, but if it feels at all cornered, it will lash out without notice. I hear you've already experienced this, yes?" Serene asked.

"Sort of, but I'd never be afraid of Embry, so she doesn't have any reason to worry about getting hurt by me."

Serene laughed. "You are not the only person in charge anymore, young wolf."

I wanted to correct the crazy lady that I wasn't a wolf, but let the inaccurate description go.

Ramona stepped forward. "As alpha female of the pack—at least until Roman takes a mate—I need to be present when Cait is trying to access the energy of the

Luna Mark. If by chance she does end up with a wolf, someone needs to be able to control her."

Embry bowed her head. "I meant no disrespect. I just know Cait, and she wouldn't have done what she did with an audience. At least now we have proof she can channel the power without being angry."

"And what proof would that be?" Serene asked.

"You didn't see it?" Embry seemed more surprised by this than I would have expected, considering she called the purple a "soft hue."

When Serene and Ramona didn't respond, Embry continued, "I had her meditate, and after about thirty minutes she was glowing purple and putting off some serious heat."

Thirty minutes? It hadn't seemed like that long when I was concentrating on myself.

Serene clapped her hands. "Well, then. Looks like I get to have some fun."

"Easy. She isn't a toy," Ramona warned.

Serene waved Ramona off. "I won't scar her."

Scarring and hurting were two completely different things. I wasn't going to be left alone with that old bitty anytime soon. Not until the evil gleam in her eyes settled down.

"What do you know about the mark that makes you want to work with Cait?" Embry asked, and I silently thanked her for having my back.

I was in way over my head at this point and glad I had someone to trust while figuring everything out. I wanted to deny fate didn't have that much control over my life, but it was a pretty big coincidence that I'd been besties with Embry and then had all of this happen to me. Even my human mind couldn't refute there were bigger things at play, at least when it came to the mark.

"I know that she has old magic in her. I know that she has the ability to choose her own destiny. I know a lot that you don't. So, don't sass me. I'm not afraid to show you my bad side."

Embry's face tried to hide a grin but failed epically. Thankfully, Serene had already moved her gaze onto me. "Show me your power."

"It doesn't have an on and off switch. I don't know how to just show you," I said as her previous words began to register with me.

There was a chance I could leave here and still lead a normal life from the sounds of it. I didn't have to choose Roman and spend the rest of my life in this pack. This gave me some peace, at least, until Serene poked my shoulder.

"Sit and meditate," she demanded, her finger a lot stronger than I expected.

Rubbing my shoulder, I placated her and sat back down. Mostly because I was curious what she and Ramona would have to say.

"Do you want me to walk you through it again?" Embry asked, standing by my side.

"No, I should be okay. It didn't take me long to figure it out," I replied and began the process.

Within minutes, or at least that's what it felt like to me, I sensed the energy before I saw it. Now that I had experienced it a couple of times, it was easier to recognize. I drew on the ball of power and sent it through my body like before, this time trying to force it through my skin.

I wasn't sure why I made that decision, but it just felt right, and given everything happening was not at all normal, I figured following my instincts was the safest bet.

Soon after I pushed harder, my muscles tightened and I lost my hold on the power. When I opened my eyes, the others were a dozen yards away and only one of them was grinning.

"What did I do?" I stood up, and they began to come closer.

"Not what you did before," Embry grumbled.

"Look at the grass around you," Serene said, and I noticed everything was brown and lifeless.

"How did I kill it?" I asked.

Ramona grimaced. "You didn't kill it. You burned the ground around you in a perfect circle. The purple flames didn't stop until we were far enough away from you."

Built-in security system. I couldn't exactly complain about that.

"That's not normal from what you know about those previously marked like me?" I asked Serene.

She shrugged. "Each one is different. There's no standard to base things off of. The only difference we haven't been able to figure out about you is that you aren't descended from shifters. At least not that we know of, but I intend to find out."

I didn't know my father, so this intrigued me. "How do you plan to do that?"

"I have a friend in L.A. She's coming here to test your bloodlines," Serene answered and did not make me feel comfortable with her statement.

"You invited Beatrix here?" Embry asked with a frown.

"Oh, calm your tits. The witch is harmless. I need to go. Don't practice without us again." Before anyone could object, the old shifter was running off as if she was still in her prime.

I didn't give her departure a second thought. I was more focused on the fact that a witch was headed here to mess with my blood, or something close to that if I understood Serene correctly.

Embry put both hands on my shoulders. "Deep breath, Cait. Focus on me and nothing else."

I did as she asked, but the normal calming effect she had on me wasn't working.

"I can't do this, Em. I'm not one of you. I don't want to be a mate. I don't want to be marked."

"I know, but we can't make the mark go away, and I think you need to understand it before you make any other decisions," Embry said, and I knew she was right. I'd had the same thoughts earlier.

The thought of witches and having purple flames igniting from my body had caused a minor, or maybe not so minor, freak-out to occur.

I nodded at her and took a shuddering breath before straightening my shoulders. "You're right. One thing at a time. Just don't introduce me to any other supernaturals. I don't think my brain can process any more right now."

Embry grinned. "Deal." She turned behind us. "Ramona, do you have anything you'd like us to do until we meet up again?"

I'd forgotten Ramona was there during my little episode and felt bad I mentioned something about not wanting to be a mate. It was her son I'd be walking away from, and that made things incredibly awkward.

She smiled softly, pushed her short blonde strands behind her ear, and met my eyes. "Serene mentioned you were interested in some books in the pack library. I brought some over to Embry's house earlier. Read those if you're still interested until Beatrix arrives. Then, we'll decide what to do next."

Reading. I'd forgotten about the books I'd intended to borrow before I'd seen Roman and Sam together. Hopefully those were the ones Ramona had brought to the house. If so, I knew exactly what I'd be doing for the rest of the day.

18

ROMAN

When Cait had walked away from me, I fought every instinct to follow her. Most females would love the attention, but Cait was different. She didn't want anything to do with me, yet I could see how much I affected her.

The inner turmoil she seemed to be going through was my only hope that I wasn't going to be left alone when she finally figured things out.

My mom must have told Dad that I'd resorted to kidnapping after Cait had told on me, because I was being summoned to his office, which wasn't actually indoors. At least, not since I'd taken over as alpha.

I found him in his favorite spot, reclining in a chair on the dock at the property pond. He took retirement very seriously.

"Hello, Son," he said before I even stepped foot on the wood planks.

"Father," I replied, going along with his serious tone and taking the seat at his side.

He cast his line and reeled it in a few feet before he was happy with the lure's placement. Only then did he turn toward me. "So, how are things?"

I grinned. "You know exactly how things are."

He tipped his head and checked his line, making minor adjustments. Like I said, he took retirement seriously. "No, I know what your mother has been going on about for the last few days, but I haven't actually gotten to have a chat with my boy. So, why don't you tell me what's been happening?"

He wasn't wrong. The only time we'd really had together since I returned home was spent going over Luna Mark research. Even then, we didn't really talk about Cait and what the bond between me and her might mean. I hadn't been ready then, and like the good alpha he always was, Dad had seemed to know.

"Well, Cait doesn't want anything to do with me. She used some of the energy of the mark today, though. I'm not sure if that will make things worse or better for us."

"You know taking her against her will doesn't help you any, Son."

"Yeah, I'm fully aware, but she's very stubborn. She thought Sam was something more than my best friend and cousin. I needed Cait to hear me out before she took off," I said.

Dad reeled in his line and recast, staying quiet as he focused on the task. "Cait is handling all of this pretty remarkably, given she knew nothing of our kind before coming here. You should be kissing Embry's feet for making this easier on you. Give Cait time and space. Let her find her footing and come to you. I saw the way she looked at you when we all had dinner. She feels something."

I grunted. "But is it enough? Like you said, she's handling this all really well, but that's what we see on the outside. I have no way to know what she's thinking, and it's killing me."

Dad set his pole down and gave me his full attention. "Nobody knows what is in another's heart. I can give you advice and hope you listen, but at the end of the day, it's up to you to make the choice you feel is best. I don't know anything about Cait. Her situation is completely unique. I just caution you to move slowly and with thoughtful actions."

I couldn't help but laugh. "Dad, it's a mate bond. I'm not the only one in control here."

"Then, I hope your wolf is listening and taking the advice to heart as well. He's waited a long time for Cait. Let's hope his animal instincts don't screw it up for the both of you."

I'm starting to not like your father, my wolf grumbled.

I ignored him and thanked my dad for his wisdom.

"No thanks needed, Son. I'm here for you whenever you need it, no matter what it's for. Besides Cait, is everything else going good within the pack and your head?"

I shrugged. "There are some murmurs about Cait,

which are causing worry within the pack, but hopefully it's nothing other than people being curious."

"Don't get too distracted with your personal life and forget about the bigger picture. I know you need to sort things out with Cait, but the pack will be watching your every move to see where your priorities lie. To them, Cait's a human with no purpose being on pack lands," he said, and I was already fully aware of that. It was why I'd been so frustrated that she was my mate to begin with.

"I'll be careful. Vaughn has his ears open as well. He's better with the peopling than me anyway." I stood up and leaned over to hug my dad. "Thanks again for the chat."

"I love you, Son."

"I love you, too."

One thing my dad had never lacked was showing affection. He'd taught me that showing care for those you loved didn't make you weak. It only proved how strong you really were. I didn't always understand his thought behind that, but I was beginning to.

Then, you need to be showing Cait all of your emotions, my wolf piped in.

I will. When the time is right.

And what if you're too late? he asked.

I'll give you full control for a month if I mess things up.

Hmm, deal. We'll do it your way for now. Just know I'll be rooting for your failure.

I snorted. *Gee, thanks.*

Talking with my dad had helped, but I still needed

to let some… frustrations out. I decided to head toward the woodshed and start chopping. My mom loved having a fire all day, every day during the winter. Even though it didn't get very cold here most days, Mom insisted the fireplace made the pack house feel more like a home.

In order to keep her happy, it took working on and off all year to build a wood supply that would heat the house for months at a time. Normally, it was a chore I delegated to wolves who needed a time out, but I was happy to give myself one today.

///

I SPENT AN HOUR SWINGING THE AXE AND WAS COMPLETELY zoned out until I heard female voices. As soon as I paused, I sensed Cait and Embry near. By the time I turned around, they were nowhere in sight.

Victory will be so sweet, my wolf said, and I ignored him.

He was insane if he thought taking over as wolf was going to win Cait over.

Instead of stressing on what they were doing, I went inside to shower before asking Paul, one of the pack guards, to stack the wood I'd chopped.

After I was done cleaning up, I wanted to see Cait. I went to Embry's house, but they weren't there. Like a stalker, I crept around to Cait's bedroom window and slid it open. I'd only done it a time or two before. Okay, maybe three times, but being around her scent calmed me in a way I badly needed.

It wasn't just my wolf who wanted her. The more interaction I had with Cait, the more I realized she was everything I would have asked for in a mate, besides the fact she couldn't shift into a wolf.

Cait was strong. I knew this from how she'd handled herself so far. Even if she'd had a few freak-outs, they were nothing in the grand scheme of things. She cared about those close to her. She was eager to learn, which made me believe she was smarter than people usually thought.

It also helped that she was sexy as hell. The first time I'd seen her on the beach wearing a black bikini and dripping wet, I nearly fell to my knees. I would have if I hadn't thought someone was trying to trick me. It had taken everything in me to resist the urge to wrap her in my arms then.

The way she'd stood up to me and walked away without care had been something I wasn't used to, but it made more sense once I realized she truly had no idea who I was.

After searching Cait's room from the window to make sure nothing was amiss and inhaling her scent, I slid the window back closed and headed out into the forest.

Want to go for a run? I asked my wolf.

You know I'll never say no to that.

He also hadn't given me hell for my stalker-like tendencies, which I appreciated.

Shifting used to bring me an enjoyable calm before Cait came around. It was my time to take a back seat and trust my wolf with control. He might be a smartass on occasion, but we had a solid partnership that allowed me to be the alpha our pack needed.

As my body shimmered and clothes faded away, I pushed the shift forward and landed on all fours within seconds. So long as a shifter was thinking about their clothes, they didn't get ruined during the transition from man to wolf.

The poor pups trying to learn when they were between four and seven years old often just ran around naked. It was equal parts entertaining and annoying.

My wolf twisted his head around and stretched his legs out. His nose went up in the air, and I could sense he wanted to let out a deep howl, but something else caught his attention.

His head snapped to the east. *What is it?* I asked.

Mine, was all he said before sprinting into the trees.

I let him do his thing, assuming he was just hunting prey until he skidded to a stop and I looked through his eyes.

Cait was sitting in the grass with my mom, Serene, and Embry standing further away from her.

What are they doing? I asked more to myself than my wolf.

We waited for what felt like forever until purple magic began to spread along Cait's skin. She didn't seem like she was in pain, so my wolf stayed put. Then, the energy got bigger and turned into flames, burning the area around her, but not marking her clothes.

Just as I was about to force my wolf to charge in, she stopped, and the others moved to her side. I wanted to be closer—thankfully, my wolf did, too—so we crept past a few more trees before laying down in the brush.

"Each one is different. There's no standard to base things off of. The only difference we haven't been able to figure out about you is that you aren't descended from shifters. At least, not that we know of, but I intend to find out," Serene said, and it made me wonder about Cait's birth family. I didn't know anything about them other than her mother died.

"How do you plan to do that?" Cait asked.

"I have a friend in L.A. She's coming here to test your bloodlines," Serene replied, causing my annoyance to rise. She hadn't asked me about inviting a witch here, and she would know that wasn't acceptable.

I missed the next few things they said until Serene took off. Hopefully, I'd find her in my office when I went back. Otherwise, she'd find me at her doorstep.

Embry put her hands on Cait's shoulders. "Deep breath, Cait. Focus on me and nothing else."

"I can't do this, Em. I'm not one of you. I don't want to be a mate. I don't want to be marked."

"I know, but we can't make the mark go away, and I think you need to understand it before you make any other decisions," Embry said, and I was more thankful than ever for her guidance to Cait.

We should give them some privacy, I said to my wolf.

We should.

But you don't want to? I asked.

Do you want to leave her after seeing what she did? he countered.

I knew where he was coming from, but Cait was having a private conversation, and it wasn't our place. My mom was still there, so I knew if there was anything dire I needed to know, she'd tell me.

Let's go, I said, and my wolf turned without argument.

19

CAIT

It had been a week since the mark appeared on my wrist and a few days since sitting in the field and finally using the power I had access to. Since then, I'd been unable to deny there was something different about me. There was a sense of peace that had formed within me, and I was able to think clearer after tapping into the energy.

Roman had also given me some space, which helped tremendously. The more I thought about him without his presence influencing me, the more certain I was that this was not the life I wanted for myself. If I was not turning into a wolf, then I wanted to live my own normal-as-possible life.

I didn't want to hurt anyone's feelings. While I couldn't deny there was a major attraction to Roman, having my future so decided just wasn't something I could live with.

When I'd lost the most important person in my

life, I vowed to myself that I would live my life the way I saw fit, which was why I'd ended up traveling for so long. I wasn't ready for my freedoms to be taken away at only twenty-one years old, but I could at least be civil while figuring out what the mark really meant.

So far, the energy was manageable. I hadn't felt out of control or overwhelmed, and Embry thought that was a really good thing. She was praising my progress, all while being unaware that the more confidence she gave me, the sooner I was going to be leaving.

I hated having this secret, but I knew she wouldn't understand. Sure, she loved me and was my best friend, but to her, this pack was life and a wonderful thing to be part of. I was glad she had it, but I didn't need it.

"What do you want to do today?" Embry asked when I came out of my room.

It had been the same thing for the last couple days. She was up before dawn working for the pack, and I'd roll out of bed whenever I wanted. Then, we'd go on some adventure to pretend we weren't working on my energy control.

Serene and Ramona hopefully had no clue we weren't listening to their warning of not practicing again without them. Both had been busy with research, but I knew the witch was supposed to arrive today.

"What time is Beatrix going to be here?" I asked.

"Not sure. She'll come by portal whenever she's ready. Could be in ten minutes or ten hours," Embry said.

"Let's just stick around here, then. A boring day indoors doesn't sound terrible, actually," I said.

Though I had enjoyed getting out around the pack property, I also missed my down time and, more than that, my alone time. I loved Embry, but the only time I was by myself was when I was in my room. Even then, she had no problem storming in with all her natural excitement at any given time. After nearly a week, it was getting to me.

"Sounds great to me." Embry's computer made some noises, and she got back to work.

I crept away, deciding a nice hot bath sounded like a great way to pass the time while she finished up.

Going back to my room, I grabbed my towel and phone so I could read a book while I soaked. I'd been reading the history books Ramona had brought over, and it reminded me I needed more fiction in my life.

Once the tub was full, I double-checked the door was locked, then undressed. As soon as I was submerged in the water, I sighed with happiness.

"This is what I've been missing," I said to myself.

Grabbing my phone, I intended to go straight to my book app, but thought maybe I would do a quick check on the outside world just to make sure the humans hadn't burned anything down while I'd been distracted with supernatural events.

I had no messages from friends. Embry was pretty much the only person I ever consistently kept in touch with. When I left my hometown, my friends from school reached out on occasion, but I pushed them away. Dealing with the grief of losing my mother seemed best to do alone or with random strangers.

I didn't know why I had no desire to count on those closest to me, but I'd found my outlets and didn't feel bad about the choices I made. Whether or not they might have been made in error, they were my mistakes to make, and as long as I had control, that was all I needed to keep moving forward.

The world was thankfully boring, from what I could tell, so I opened the book I'd last been checking out. The page I'd read last was the lead-up to a steamy scene I'd been waiting on for two books. The angst with this series was real. Just as things were coming to a head, Embry pounded on the door, scaring the hell out of me.

"What?" I snapped, thankful I hadn't dropped my phone in the water.

"Beatrix is here," she replied.

Go fucking figure. Irritation flooded through me as I set my phone down. I would finish the chapter later that night when I'd be least likely to be interrupted.

"I'll be out in a minute," I grumbled.

I unplugged the drain before drying off. I hadn't brought any clean clothes into the bathroom with me, so I wrapped the fluffy towel around my body and stepped into the hallway. I glanced over to ask Embry something, but the words were lost on me when Ramona, Jack, Roman, and a woman I assumed to be Beatrix were standing in the entryway.

Oh, this day was not going to be what I hoped for.

Owning the situation, I waved. "How's it going?"

Roman's eyes bored into me, but I ignored him, trying not to lose my composure.

"Cait, dear. Why don't you get dressed and we'll wait outside until you're ready," Ramona said as Jack wrapped a hand around Roman's shoulder.

I nodded and walked to my room, closing the door and leaning against it. My heart was beating like crazy, and my skin warmed. Looking down at my mark, I noticed it was still the same size, but seemed to be changing colors. It was a dark brown now, and I wondered what was causing the variations.

Too bad there wasn't time to ask if anyone knew why. I had to go meet a witch about my blood. Totally normal.

It was still hot as Satan's house outside, so I dressed in shorts and a t-shirt before deciding to leave my hair in a messy bun. I wasn't trying to impress anyone. Though, I was enjoying the golden hue my skin was taking on from all the sunshine I'd been soaking in.

Embry was waiting for me at my door. "I'm so sorry. I tried to get them to wait outside, but Beatrix insisted they wait inside until you came out. I didn't want to get on her bad side. Witches like to hold grudges."

"It's alright. Let's just get this over with and see if we can salvage the day after she's gone," I replied.

By the time we joined them outside, Serene had arrived as well. Great. I was going to be their entertainment for the day.

I avoided looking at Roman. I'd already made up my mind during our time apart and didn't want lines to get blurred or to lead him on. Maybe after Beatrix was done with her witchy stuff and we knew more, I could tell Embry and Roman my intentions.

Beatrix looked much too old to… well, I didn't know what she was going to do, but she seemed more like a grandma than a powerful witch. She was wearing a long dark coat and a one-piece navy-blue outfit. She had long grey hair that reminded me of Serene's, as well as a face full of wrinkles.

It was Beatrix's eyes that took me by surprise. There was nothing old about them. They were a bright emerald, and something about them screamed mischief. I would be listening to her words carefully in hopes of not being deceived.

"Come closer, child," Beatrix said, and I caught the twitch of Roman's arm from the corner of my eye, but he stayed where he stood several feet away.

Embry nudged me forward, and I placed my hand in Beatrix's waiting one. She wrapped her fingers around my palm and then moved further up my wrist to the mark.

Her eyes closed, and I glanced at Embry, hoping for some sort of confirmation this was normal. While I was turned away, Beatrix pulled a blade from what I thought was thin air and sliced into my palm.

"The hell?" I yanked my hand back and hissed at her. "Was that necessary?"

"Would you have rather I asked first?" she replied.

Maybe she sort of had a point, but I wasn't going to agree.

The crazy witch stuck the dagger in a pouch. "Give me your hand and I'll heal you."

I was hesitant. She was a witch, and the possibilities of what she could do to me were endless—most of which were likely not good. When I didn't give her my hand, she took it, then turned to Serene. "Do you have somewhere I can work?"

"You can come to my house," Serene replied.

I breathed a sigh of relief as I felt the wound closing. Maybe she wouldn't turn me into a frog.

She released me but stayed close. "I have a theory, and I don't think my results will be accurate without testing something. I'd like you to spend the next little while with Roman and I'll retest things after you're done."

Yep. This day was definitely not going as planned.

"I thought you were here to test my bloodlines," I challenged.

"I am. I thought you might like other answers based on what Serene told me. I don't often assume wrong," Beatrix answered.

I didn't reply, because she was right. I did want to know more. I wanted it more than anything else. Except, spending the next little while with Roman seemed like a big ask. I knew it shouldn't be if I was so ready to walk away, but I was afraid the bond would change my mind. Afraid I would lose control over my decisions.

Beatrix began to leave with Serene, and Embry

looped her arm through mine. "Don't worry about anything. We'll have fun all hanging out together."

Beatrix called back to us. "No. Only Cait and Roman, at least for now. I have theories I need to test."

The sneering smile she sent our way made my blood go cold. Who the hell was this woman? Well, she wasn't a woman, for one. She was a witch, and I needed to remember that. For a brief moment, I'd thought she wouldn't be as scary as I'd first believed the wolves were, but I was dead wrong.

Roman appeared at my side. "Don't threaten my mate, Beatrix. Remember whose land you're on."

"And remember, it's my help you need to figure out what she is," the witch countered before stalking off again.

Serene mouthed an apology and followed after her friend.

"I hate witches almost as much as I do the bloodsuckers," Embry grumbled, then turned to me. "Are you okay with this?"

I wanted answers. Even though I didn't want them this way, I didn't seem to have a choice for the time being. I just needed to steel my resolve and remember what I wanted most. I knew what that was. I'd been repeating it for the last few days. Freedom was my end game, not a mate.

"Yeah, I'll be fine. See you in a few hours," I said before looking at Roman. "Where to?"

His chest rose and fell, slowing as his rage from

Beatrix's threat seemed to calm. It was hard not to appreciate his protectiveness.

"The cabin if you're okay with it," he replied.

"We're just a shout away if you two need anything. Hopefully by the end of the day, all of this will make a little more sense," Ramona said as Jack took her hand.

"Stay close, Son," Jack added.

Roman nodded at his parents as they walked away. Embry was also gone, and it was just me and the man who wanted me as his mate.

Nothing awkward at all.

20

CAIT

For the first time, Roman let me walk to where we were going instead of picking me up and running at impossible speeds. The path to his cabin was filled with awkward silence, but I tried to pay more attention to our surroundings than I did him.

It didn't work as well as I would have liked.

Roman opened the door for me to his cabin, and I went in, thankful that nearly thirty minutes had already passed with how slow I'd been walking.

"Do you spend a lot of time here?" I asked as he shut the door.

"Not usually. My pack relies on me for certain things, but it's also nice to have my own space when I need it."

I understood that. It was why I wanted to leave. I was only twenty-one. I still had so much living to do before I settled down.

I sat down in the only available chair, wanting to

stay away from the bed, and tried to think of anything else to talk about.

The last time I was with Roman, I'd been irritated with him. It was easier to argue with him than whatever was happening between us currently.

"How have things been working with Embry?" Roman asked, sitting on the edge of his bed and facing me.

We were a good six feet from each other, but I could still feel the heat rolling from his body. Then, I pictured him chopping wood and forgot what he asked me. I was never going to make it a couple of hours. This was so bad.

"Sorry, I've got a lot on my mind. What did you ask?" I mumbled.

He smiled. "I asked how things are going working with Embry. Are you controlling the energy more?"

I wanted to question how he knew I'd been working on it at all, but remembered he was the pack alpha. He probably didn't have to twist arms too hard to get the information he wanted.

"It's going well, actually. The first day was a bit much, but I'm not burning anything down, so that's a good thing," I said.

He didn't seem surprised by my comment about burning things. Ramona must have already told him how the first session went.

"I'm glad. Is there anything you planned to work on today? We could do it together if you wanted," Roman added.

"Today was going to be a day off, but thanks for offering," I replied.

He nodded, and we were back to awkward silence. It was as if he knew I was planning to leave or something, but then again, I remembered how he'd come to my side when Beatrix threatened me and how he'd reacted when I stepped out of the bathroom.

I was more than confused on how to read Roman, but hopefully it wouldn't be something I had to worry about for much longer.

A few minutes later, after I'd already begun counting the wood slats in the ceiling, he spoke up again. "Do you want to go down to the creek?"

"Sure, why not." Roman didn't have a TV in the cabin, and I didn't see any books, so anything else was better than sitting there. I should have grabbed my phone so I could read, but reading the next few scenes with Roman near probably wasn't a great idea either.

We walked the hundred-or-so feet to the creek, and I watched Roman as he picked up a flat rock and skipped it across the slow-moving surface.

"I used to do that all the time as a kid," I said, remembering my mom teaching me how. She took her role as both mother and father very seriously, something that I did my best to never take for granted.

Roman tossed a rock at me and grinned. "Let's see what you got."

I wasn't one to back down, so I moved closer to the water's edge and frowned when my rock sunk into the water without skipping. Apparently, rock skipping was a talent that one lost if they didn't keep up with it.

"Come on. I'll help you try again." Roman handed me another rock but didn't let go of my hand once I had hold of it.

He moved around behind me and drew my arm back. All the while, his chest was pressed firmly against my back and his other hand was loosely holding on to my hip. This felt too intimate, but I couldn't deny the closeness made my heart race in a good way.

"Hold the rock only with your thumb and index finger at the two ends, then turn it at a bit of an angle like this." His grip on my hip tightened as he guided me. "Keep your hand below your shoulder and concentrate on throwing fast, but not hard."

Oh, something was definitely hard.

My face blushed, and I was thankful he was behind me. Taking a deep breath, I steadied myself and tried to forget Roman was holding me so close. I pulled my arm further back and released the stone.

Watching the water's surface, I clapped when the rock made it halfway across the creek with two skips. "It worked!"

He turned me around, his hands cupping my jawline, and I sucked in a breath. Jesus, my restraints were no match for this kind of sex appeal.

"Cait, I need to…" His sentence trailed off as he lowered his head.

I had plenty of time to stop him. I knew I should. I almost did. I was so close to saying the words.

Yet, I didn't.

Selfishly, I accepted his movements and kissed him back, taking whatever he had to offer for the moment. Roman sucked on my lower lip, opening my mouth before gliding his tongue in, sliding one hand around the base of my neck and the other to my lower back.

I was locked against him and gripped his shirt as I let his mouth devour mine. Our tongues fought for control as I moaned against him. My skin heated, and my heart raced, but none of that was as strong as the sexual build-up.

My legs pressed together as he pushed me closer, and I tried to fight the growing ache. My hands flattened on his chest, and I pushed back. "Roman," I murmured.

He trailed kisses down my jaw and focused on my neck. "Hmmm."

Damn, he was not making this easy. I was either the biggest idiot in the world, or the strongest woman alive for what I was about to do next—likely the former.

"Please, stop."

My words had the desired effect, except when Roman moved back, I instantly missed his warmth and hated that.

"You don't want this?" he asked.

"This shouldn't happen," I said instead of answering.

He raised an eyebrow. "And why is that?"

"Because I don't want it to."

He grunted with a smirk. "That's not what it felt like to me."

"Roman, don't make this harder than it needs to be. I'm not a wolf. I shouldn't be your mate."

"But you are mine."

"No, I'm not. I'm my own person. I don't belong to anyone," I replied, beginning to get annoyed, which was better than my previous feelings.

He stepped closer, lifting my wrist. "The moment this mark appeared, life as you knew it was over, Cait. I'm not trying to be an asshole, but you need to accept that you're not human anymore or things are only going to get more difficult."

I pushed away from him once again, this time with more force as my energy began to swirl. "Oh, yeah? For who? Me? Or are you only worried about you?"

"That's not what I meant. I can protect you here. I can give you as normal of a life as possible within this pack, but out in the world, nothing will be the same as it was before, no matter how much you want it to be."

I crossed my arms and inched further away. "And how can you possibly know that?"

He sighed, clearly annoyed with me. "Because you're not human. How many times do we have to tell you that? You're marked in a shifter world, and unable to properly protect yourself right now. You're unclaimed *and* unattached. Naturally, other supernaturals will be curious, and that type of interest isn't likely to be a good thing."

His words had their desired effect. Fear slammed

into me as the truth of them hit me like a truck. That same fear was making me act without reason and push everyone away. A part of me knew I shouldn't, but I was scared beyond reason and the constant reminder that everything had changed in my life was not helping. Not one damn bit. I needed more time to find some steady ground to stand on without feeling as if everything was spiraling around me.

"I can't do this right now, Roman. I need to focus on one thing at a time, and you're not number one on my list of priorities right now. I am. And what this mark means for me."

My mother had always taught me to be brave and independent. I was pretty sure this wasn't how she saw my life turning out and I was lost. In the years since she'd been gone, never before had I missed her as much as I did now.

Roman growled and turned away from me as he ran his fingers through his hair. I took the moment to walk away as well, but I wasn't going to stay close. I didn't care what Beatrix said. My time with Roman needed to be up before I lost hold of my emotions. I was going to find wherever Serene lived. There had to be something they could tell me.

Knowing Roman wouldn't let me get far, I began to run. My legs were stiff. Sprinting wasn't something I'd done since high school, but the longer my strides got, the easier the pacing became. I was running faster than ever before, but not like Roman did.

I was so intrigued by this new ability that I wasn't

paying close attention to what was in front of me and slammed into a hard force. I landed on my ass with an audible thud and barely stopped my head from slamming into the dirt ground.

A man stood over me and reached his hand out. "Sorry, miss. I didn't see you there."

I took his offered help, but as soon as his fingers wrapped around my palm, an uneasiness settled within my stomach. I acted like I had to brush myself off and took a few steps back to get a look at him.

I was certain I'd never seen him before. He had obsidian hair, cropped short, with russet eyes and a sharp chin. He was tall, but not much over six feet.

"Are you okay?" he asked while appraising me.

"Yep. I just needed the reminder to slow down and pay attention. Reminder received," I said and started to walk away.

The guy moved into my path. "What's your name? I haven't seen you around here before."

"If you don't already know who I am, then you probably don't need to," I replied without thinking twice about the repercussions. Assuming this dude was a shifter, I probably shouldn't antagonize him. "I'm sorry. I really need to go."

"Oh, come on. I'm Kyle." He reached a hand to me, but I ignored it.

"I really need to go," I repeated with more force behind my words as I moved to sidestep him, but he grabbed on to my wrist, squeezing tight.

"Now you're just being rude. Tell me your name," he seethed as his grip strengthened.

The power I'd been working to control was there, but something told me I was better off kneeing this guy in the balls than showing him what I was capable of.

"Let her go," Roman's voice bellowed from behind.

Kyle did just that, but didn't move away. "Calm down, dear cousin. I was just trying to meet your new pack member. Interesting that you haven't registered her on the pack list."

"She and my pack are none of your damned business. Now, what do you want?"

I moved closer to Roman as they traded words, curious to know where this guy was from, considering he'd called Roman his cousin.

"I just came here for a little chat, but I can see you're busy. I'll go make myself comfortable in the main house. Maybe I'll find my auntie."

The way "auntie" rolled off his tongue made my stomach churn. Whoever he was to the pack and Roman's family, I instinctively knew he was bad news and hoped he didn't stick around long.

"We can all walk back together," Roman said through gritted teeth.

"Or perhaps run? The female is quite fast." Kyle licked his lips as he took another close look at me.

Roman didn't do anything to defend me, which surprised the hell out of me. Maybe I'd finally gotten my point across.

"Running it is. After you," Roman said to Kyle, who smirked at each of us before taking off.

Roman said nothing to me as we followed. Kyle was almost out of eyesight. My pace was not keeping up with the wolf's, but Roman stayed with me. For that, I was thankful.

By the time we got back to the pack house, Kyle was likely already inside, and Embry was waiting for me.

She wrapped me in her arms. "I'm so glad you're okay."

"Why wouldn't I be?" I asked.

"We'll talk about it later. Come on." She pulled on my hand and nodded at Roman as he stomped toward the pack house without giving me another glance.

21

CAIT

Just as we began to walk away, Kyle whistled, getting our attention from across the driveway. "Bring the girl. I'd like to get to know her better."

Roman snarled. "She doesn't have any business in a meeting between our packs."

Kyle grinned. "Oh, something tells me otherwise, cousin."

Roman calmed himself and shrugged. "Whatever. She isn't mine to control and doesn't mean anything to me. Just don't touch my pack members. You know the rules."

"Without their permission, of course." Kyle licked his lips, and I vomited a little in my mouth.

Roman saying that I didn't mean anything to him stung more than I expected, considering I wanted to be left alone. I ignored the feeling and headed toward the pack house instead of Embry's.

She was right at my side, grabbing my arm. "Don't say anything and keep your arms at your sides."

"Two for one? My lucky day," Kyle said when we approached the steps.

"If you want a meeting, show some damn respect before I kick you off my land," Roman said. His gaze avoided mine but met Embry's on several occasions.

Roman led the way to one of the offices I'd seen on my previous tour. It was the biggest one with a table meant for a dozen people. Embry stood at the wall with me at her side until Kyle sat. Then, we took the furthest seats from him.

I kept my arms under the table, and Embry let go of me. "It's been a while, Kyle. How are things on the west side?" Embry asked casually.

"If you're so curious, you should come back with me and I can show you," he replied.

This guy was ridiculous. It was hard to believe he was somehow related to Roman.

"What do you want?" Roman asked, settling his hands on the tabletop a little harder than necessary.

"Well, that changes by the moment, but Cohen sent me here to ask about the Tuttle acreage. We'd like to use it, given it hasn't been touched in decades and borders our property line. He's willing to pay," Kyle said.

Roman scoffed. "Not a chance in hell. You didn't honestly come here for that. He would have already known the answer. We don't need money, so the offer to buy means nothing to us. Cohen must be losing his wit in his old age."

"Don't disrespect family, Roman. It isn't polite," Kyle said.

"Family? Cohen hasn't ever been that to me. The only ones I consider family live within my pack." Roman stared Kyle down, waiting for a reaction that never came.

"Good to know. I'll remind you of that when your way of thinking bites you in the ass. Grandfather hoped that maybe you'd be smarter than your father, but I can see that's not the case," Kyle said.

"You'd do well to remember where you are. Insult my father and I will do more than kick you off my land," Roman replied, his hand tightening into a fist.

Kyle turned his gaze toward me. "What are you?" he asked.

I glanced at Embry and Roman, having no idea how to respond. They'd both said people would sense the magic within me, so I couldn't say I was human.

Embry saved me by answering first. "She's a guest of mine and none of your business."

Kyle sniffed the air, leaning closer across the table. "I bet you're part fae. Don't see them too much around here. I'd loved to know what the other half of you is."

"She's human and fae. Nothing worth writing home about. Embry befriended her, and she's only here a short time. You're welcome to question her, but someone wiped her memory, so good luck," Roman said in a monotone voice.

My cheeks flushed with mixed emotions, and I kept my mouth shut. I might not want to stay here, but I trusted Embry and she trusted Roman. Whatever they were saying was fine with me.

"Interesting. Where will you go after this?" Kyle asked, staring at me.

"I like to travel. So, who knows? Could be anywhere," I answered honestly, because at the moment, that was my plan. When lying, I'd learned it was best to stick as close to the truth as possible.

"Hmm. Pity," Kyle said and stood up, glancing at Roman. "Given you're being just as obstinate as your father, I guess I'll be going now."

I breathed a sigh of relief that he wasn't going to take Roman up on his offer and question me. Embry stayed seated and I did, too, but my relief was short-lived. Kyle approached us and held his hand out. "It was nice to meet you. Oh, wait. I didn't catch your name."

Embry shook his hand. "Her name is Julie."

"Julie. Rolls off the tongue nicely," he said as Embry pulled her hand back, but he waited for me to do the same. The mark was on my left wrist so I was safe to shake with my regular hand, but before I could give him a firm grip, he took my fingers and brought my hand close to his lips.

"I hope we meet again, Julie."

I smiled at him, but it probably came out as more of a sneer as he kissed my skin.

Embry stood, making more noise than necessary as she did so. "Well, safe travels back, Kyle."

He released his hold on me. "It's a pity I'll be doing it alone."

Neither of us replied to that comment, and I didn't realize until he and Roman disappeared into the hallway that I was shaking.

As soon as we were alone, the mark flared, and I pulled my other arm out.

"Calm down, Cait. He needs to be off pack land before you lose control," Embry warned.

I wasn't trying to lose control, but the mark seemed to have a mind of its own. I focused on breathing and clearing my thoughts. Kyle was leaving. I was safe. Everything was fine.

"Good job. Now, let's go," Embry said.

We both got up and went toward the kitchen, using the back door to exit the house. I assumed we were headed to her house, but she walked toward Vaughn's.

Still, we didn't stop there and continued on past, walking at a near run. "Is everything okay, Em?"

"We need to get you back to Serene and Beatrix. Serene has been calling for you since we got back to the pack house, but we couldn't just walk out of the meeting. Kyle would have pushed for information. Unfortunately, the fact that he didn't means he saw what he was looking for, but I have no idea what that was."

"Why couldn't Roman have just told him I was off limits?" I asked.

"Because if we made any big deal about you or being around him, he would have been even more curious, and that's not good for anyone. We're just lucky Kyle found you alone and not with Roman. You're not ready for the public to know you're his mate," she said.

"And why is that?" I knew why *I* didn't, but assumed it wasn't the same as her thoughts.

"When a powerful alpha with a large territory claims a mate, people take notice. They want to know if it's a true mate, how the bonding might shift power control, and whether the mate is worthy. This is an old school way of thinking, and most packs don't give a shit, but there are some that do, like the one next door and a few others."

I didn't really want the answer to my next question, but I needed to know. "And what if people don't find me worthy?"

"Then, you might be threatened or Roman could be challenged for the pack's control," Embry answered.

"What about if we never mate?" I asked, because I'd already read that a bond wasn't complete until the shifters had sex, regardless if they were true mates. I still had the opportunity to walk away with my sanity intact.

"Roman would have to get over the fact that he would never be with his true mate and then find someone else. Most shifters don't go actively looking for love, but as alpha, if he knows a true mate isn't an option, he'll need to find someone worthy enough. Otherwise, he still faces the risk of being challenged for the pack's control. Did Roman tell you why Cohen was so pissed Ramona mated with Jack?" she asked.

"No, just that it wasn't an easy time for them," I said.

"Cohen had gotten himself into some trouble with another pack. To save his own ass, he promised Ramona to their alpha. When Jack turned out to be her true mate, the other alpha left Ramona alone but still went after Cohen. The west territory has never recovered from those consequences. The shifters not mated or deeply rooted in the land left, which were mostly women. Their pack is slowly dying out, and Cohen has been trying to take over our territory ever since. Jack ruined Cohen's standing within the wolf community, and Cohen has been fighting—and failing—to get back to the top ever since."

This was just another reason I was ready to walk away from all of it. I didn't want to be in the middle of a feud between packs. I wasn't cut out for this kind of stuff.

Before I had to think of a reply, we arrived at a cabin identical to Embry's, but it had colorful flowers planted around the edges of the house.

Embry knocked on the door and Serene answered. "About damn time. What was Kyle doing here?"

"Being nosy. I'm sure there was an ulterior motive, but I couldn't figure out what. Hopefully, Roman did," Embry answered as we moved inside.

Beatrix was standing at the table with several bowls in front of her. "Where is the mate?" she asked.

"He got tied up," Embry answered.

Beatrix looked at me. "How much time did you spend with him?"

"Almost an hour."

"Did you get close to him?" she asked, and my cheeks blushed. "That's answer enough for me. Come here."

"You're going to tell me all about that when we're done here." Embry snickered as I moved toward the witch.

I most certainly was not.

Beatrix took my blood again. This time, I knew the blade was coming and looked away while she did her thing. She healed me again without asking, and I thanked her even though she'd caused the injury.

"How long until you know something?" Embry asked as I stepped back.

Beatrix didn't answer. She dipped the blood-soaked dagger into one of the pots, then swirled it around. Purple smoke filtered into the air, moving in slow circles. She then stirred the other two pots and spooned some of the liquid from each into a fourth one.

As she did, the smoke lessened from the first bowl and changed colors on the last, going from blue to green to fuchsia. "What does that mean?" I asked.

Beatrix held up a hand, not answering any questions. She was starting to annoy me, but I was smart enough to keep my thoughts to myself.

Minutes later, there was no more smoke, and Beatrix finally looked at me. "I won't know your bloodline until after I'm back home. Ancestral tracking isn't something that can be done quickly, but you're definitely not human."

"That's super helpful. Thank you so much." My words dripped with sarcasm.

"But you're also not a wolf shifter," she added.

"How can she be Roman's true mate if she's not a shifter?" Embry asked.

Beatrix smirked. "I never said she wasn't a shifter. Just not a wolf."

"What does that mean?" I asked.

The witch didn't answer right away. Instead, she focused again on the bowls and dipped her fingers into the one that put off the purple smoke. "You have the magic of a shifter, but you do not contain an animal within you. I've only heard legends of such a being before." She paused and lifted a finger covered in my blood to her mouth.

Oh, God. She was going to taste it. There were a lot of things I'd felt like I'd done a good job at accepting, but this was not going to be one of them.

Sure enough, Beatrix licked her crimson fingertips and hummed. "So much pure energy. You're lucky I'm a good witch."

"What are the stories, and what do they have to do with Cait?" Embry asked.

"Centuries ago, it's said that a being existed who could shift into any animal. Their soul was not bound to one and they lived without a pack, protecting the humans until a group of dark supernaturals attacked the being and stole the energy for themselves," Beatrix answered.

"Did this being die?" I asked.

"Nobody knows. Like I said, these are just legends. We don't even know if the being was a woman or man, but your blood was even stronger after being with Roman, so I'm not certain this is what you could be."

"Wouldn't stronger be better?" Embry asked.

Beatrix shook her head. "Not stronger as in more powerful, but as in Cait felt more like a wolf than anything else. I assume if she stays with Roman, then she will gravitate toward your wolf ways, and if she chooses not, then she's in for the fight of her life."

The way the witch spoke about me as if I wasn't there should have pissed me off, but I couldn't focus on anger.

"Is there a way to get the energy out of me?" I asked, trying not to sound hopeful.

"With the right setting, there's a possibility, but you can't take power from someone without consequence. I would have to absorb it, and that's not something I need to deal with right now," Beatrix answered.

"Wouldn't it only make you stronger?" Embry asked.

"A smart witch knows that stronger isn't always better. I have no desire to draw that kind of attention. I prefer the slow build and to keep my business my own."

"But someone else could. Someone could find me

and take the energy, then do whatever they wanted," I said as a realization I didn't care for set in.

Beatrix nodded. "They could and, if they weren't careful, there's no guarantee you'd survive. Mixing witch and shifter magic isn't recommended, for many reasons that usually end with death. If you want me to figure out another solution as to where your energy goes, I'll be happy to test some theories, but as I said, you might not like the results."

Yeah, I bet she'd have been ecstatic to make me her guinea pig. Too bad for the witch, I didn't feel like testing fate when it came to my life.

As much as I didn't want to be supernatural, I also didn't want to be dead.

22

ROMAN

Pretending Cait meant nothing to me was harder than I thought it would be, but I knew it was going to be necessary as soon as I saw Kyle. What hurt me the most, though, was how I'd gotten no reaction out of Cait when I did so.

There wasn't a sign of hurt on her face when I'd said she was nothing. It was as if my opinion of her meant nothing, and that was worse than what I expected.

I wanted to kill Kyle for touching Cait, but starting a war between our two territories was the last thing we needed. I had no doubt our pack would come out on top, but we'd still lose in ways none of us wanted to deal with.

"You're smart to send that fae mutt off. Those bastards are tricky supes. You should watch your back," Kyle said, and I let out a bitter laugh.

"I appreciate the concern."

He shrugged. "You know, if you trusted us and we

worked together, our wolves could be the most powerful in the world."

"And why would I need to be the most powerful?" I asked.

"Do you not fear being challenged again?" he countered.

"You mean am I afraid my own grandfather will try to have me killed again? If Cohen wants to keep coming for our territory, I'll be here to protect it. You're welcome to remind him of that when you run on home," I said, keeping my voice even. Kyle wanted to rile me. He wanted to know he could get under my skin, but I wouldn't give him the satisfaction of knowing he was anything but an annoyance.

Kyle grinned. "Oh, I'll be sure to tell him of everything I've seen while I've been here."

"And how long has that been?" I asked.

We had a group of guards that circled the lands we occupied most but relied on video surveillance and motion sensors that alerted us to any movements. It was the only downside to having so much territory to protect. There were a lot of ways for people to get through.

"Oh, not long. Now, where is Auntie Mo Mo?" Kyle asked, using my mother's childhood name. One she despised to this day, because her father had always called her that.

"She's busy. I think it's time for you to leave," I said.

"Who's busy? Me?" Sam's voice called from the stairs.

Kyle stiffened. He and Sam had history, and not the wholesome, family kind.

"Nice to see you, Kyle. How's the arm?" Sam asked as she joined me at my side.

"Better than ever. How's your mouth? Still in need of—" Kyle said, but she cut him off.

"If you want to keep your balls attached, I wouldn't finish that sentence," Sam warned.

Kyle winked at me. "Might be worth it."

Sam lunged for him, and I grabbed on to her arms. "Definitely not worth it," I said to her.

She snarled at him. "One of these days, I'm going to teach you a lesson you won't be able to forget."

"I look forward to it, sweetheart." Kyle blew her a kiss before walking out the door.

Sam turned to me. "Let me kill him. Please."

"Not today. Not on our pack lands. Find him in a dark alley and he's all yours," I said, moving to follow Kyle. I didn't want eyes off of him until he was long gone.

I need the guards in the woods. I want updates every minute until this piece of shit is off our land, I said to Vaughn mentally.

Already on it, boss. I called in everyone, and we've got wolves every half mile on the road leading out of here, and each one will move ahead as Kyle passes. We won't let him out of our sight, Vaughn replied.

Where did he come in at? I asked since Kyle had found us in the forest area.

Southwest corner and down the county road. Came in on

foot and knew where all the sensors were or got lucky. We'll be moving them tonight and adding another dozen, Vaughn replied.

"Kyle?" I called out as he nearly reached the woods.

He turned back but didn't say anything.

"The next time you come on my property uninvited, I will treat you as a trespasser. This is the only warning you'll get."

He shook his head. "That's no way to treat family, Roman. As I said before, it's bound to bite you in the ass. Just remember I tried to warn you as well."

"About what?"

"About turning your back on blood," he replied before shifting and racing off into the trees.

Something wasn't right, but I didn't know what. We needed to prepare for another challenge, or possibly a bigger fight. Cohen wanted something from our pack, and I wasn't going to give it to him.

My mother was just joining Sam as I turned around. "What did he want?" she asked.

"Not sure. Asked about the Tuttle property and you several times, actually," I replied.

Mom glanced past me, toward the tree line, and whispered, "Did he see her?"

"Unfortunately, *Julie* was around. He knew she was a fae hybrid," I answered louder than necessary.

Sam laughed. "Well, at least he's smarter than he looks."

"The sooner she's gone, the better. How long does

Embry expect to keep her here?" Mom asked, and I was glad they were all catching on.

When we were in human form, our hearing only went so far, but in wolf form, it stretched for miles if we wanted. Kyle could still be listening, and this was the smartest play to keep him from coming back anytime soon.

"Just another few days from the sounds of it," I answered before gesturing for all of us to go inside.

Beatrix tested Cait's blood again. Is Kyle gone? Embry's voice sounded in my head.

Vaughn is giving updates by the minute. He's almost at the south edge of the property. Stay where you are. I'll come to you, I replied.

We should have hunted him and tore his throat out for touching what's ours, my wolf hissed.

That would have only brought war and you know it, I replied.

But I would have felt better.

I sighed. *Only temporarily, I promise you that.*

He huffed in reply and quieted down.

Once we were back inside, I turned to my mother and Sam. "I want the two of you to stay inside until Kyle is far from here. He came here for more than one reason and I don't like that he was asking about you, Mom."

"I'm not afraid of them. I've stood up to Cohen plenty of times and I'll do it again. He won't ever get what he wants from this pack," she answered.

"Damn right, he won't. Why didn't you get me

when Kyle got here?" My dad came from the hallway. "I can smell him in the house."

"Listen, I handled it and I don't have time for more questions right now. I need to get to Serene's and see Cait," I said, trying not to let the anxiety choke me from being away from her and knowing Kyle was still so close.

"Go find your mate, Son. We'll catch up soon. I've got things here," Dad said.

I nodded and headed out the back door, shifting as soon as my feet hit the grass. *Run,* I told my wolf, and he had no problem complying.

By the time I got to Serene's cabin, Beatrix was gone, which only slightly disappointed me. Hopefully, Embry asked enough questions before the witch disappeared.

When my eyes landed on Cait's, I wanted nothing more than to wrap her in my arms, but then I remembered I was in my wolf form and she'd never seen me this way.

They were standing outside, and I slowed down, trotting for Cait.

She tensed up, and I hated that she was afraid.

"It's just Roman," Embry said.

"Oh," was all Cait said, but she didn't run away, so I moved closer to her, wondering if she'd treat me differently in this form.

Of course she will. I'm more handsome than you, my wolf said.

I couldn't deny that my wolf was striking. Not

because I was cocky, but because of the two-tone color of his coat. He was a rich silver on top, and the underneath fur was an ebony color. Most wolves were only one color with offsetting markings. My wolf enjoyed being unique.

He nudged her hand, forcing it on top of his head.

"Oh, that's softer than I expected," Cait said, making Embry and Serene laugh.

Cait's hand stroked my wolf's head, and he wrapped his body around her. *Don't push her,* I warned, not wanting to scare Cait.

My wolf ignored me, and I tried not to be irritated when she dug her fingers into his coat and gave him a good scratch. A rumble left his chest, and Cait jumped back.

"What was that?" she asked, pressing herself against the house.

"You ruin any of my flowers and you're going to find a different reason to be scared," Serene huffed, shooing Cait away from the precious garden.

Alright, she's had enough, I said to my wolf as I took back control.

He relented easily, and I was back on two legs within seconds. "Sorry about that. He was excited."

My wolf growled at me. *Don't make me sound like a child. I'm centuries old.*

Yeah, that isn't going to help your case, either, I replied, trying to keep the smile off my face.

Cait's eyes were wide. "You just… changed."

"Would you have rather I stayed a wolf?" I asked.

"No. I mean, I don't care. That was just, well, unexpected," she replied.

"Cait hasn't seen anyone shift yet," Embry added.

I wanted to tell her Cait needed to get used to it, but I already knew she was trying to pull away from me. No reason to let my frustrations push her further away by talking down to her.

Though, a part of me already knew Cait had made up her mind. I just wasn't done trying to prove that part wrong.

23

CAIT

What in the actual fuckery? I hadn't been prepared for Roman to be a wolf one minute and man in the next. My eyes blinked rapidly, trying to understand what I'd seen.

I'd been admiring his remarkable silver fur that was coarse on top and surprisingly soft underneath, then the next moment, I was pressed against the cabin without thinking my actions through.

A growl had slipped from the wolf, and I'd thought I'd done something wrong, but now that I'd had a minute to think about it, maybe that had been his way of purring like a cat.

After that, the wolf had started to shimmer, and I heard bones pop while my eyes tried to focus on all the things happening in just a couple of seconds. Fur disappeared, replaced by skin, and then clothes. I tried to remind myself I needed to be grateful that Roman wasn't naked, but it was harder than I liked.

He stepped toward me cautiously with his hands relaxed at his sides. "Tell me what happened with Beatrix."

The change in conversation was welcome, but also reminded me of my limited options. Basically, death or arranged marriage. I was having a great day.

"She said I'm a shifter, but I don't have an animal and there's a chance I could take the form of a different species if I chose to be on my own," I said.

"Chose? Like if you left the pack?" he asked as his kissable lips downturned. Damn him for being sexy.

"Yes," I answered, my chest rising and falling rapidly as he moved closer.

"But if she leaves the pack, she could have the power within her sucked out and possibly die," Serene added, and I glared at her. "If he's going to know, he needs to know everything."

She wasn't wrong, but I wouldn't have worded it so callously. I already knew Roman was an overprotective man. If he had any idea I wanted to leave, he'd never let me out of his sight, and I wasn't going to be a prisoner here.

Embry joined my side, wrapping her arm around my waist. "Cait isn't going anywhere. These are all just assumptions. Beatrix couldn't be certain what Cait is, and to me that's a good thing. If a witch as powerful as her didn't figure it out and Kyle assumed that she was fae, then it means we have a chance at keeping her safe. That's what's most important here."

Roman nodded. "Yes. You're right, Embry." He took a step back and met my eyes. "So, you'll stay?"

I didn't want to lie to him. There was a physical ache within my chest at the thought of doing so. "For now," I answered, because that was all I could promise.

The frown lines on his face deepened, but he didn't push the subject.

"It's been a day, and I'm getting tired. If we're all done here, I'd like to go rest," I said. My mind was spent, and I had a lot to think about after Beatrix's ominous words.

"I was hoping we could work together today," Serene said.

"Tomorrow?" I replied, and she nodded. "I'll be here first thing in the morning."

"How about afternoon? I take my beauty sleep very seriously," she said without cracking a smile.

"That works for me." I could get more reading done in the morning while Embry worked.

Roman stared at me, seeming to want to say something.

"Yes?" I asked.

He shifted his feet around. "I just wanted to make sure you knew I only said those things earlier because of Kyle. There was no truth to them."

I smiled at him. "I figured."

Roman nodded, then Embry pulled me along. "Want to run? I heard you acquired some speed."

I groaned. "Not particularly."

She nudged me. "Come on. It's not actual exercise if it's easy."

She was right about that. I hadn't even been out of breath when we'd gotten back to the pack house earlier. While I wasn't fond of working out, running hadn't seemed hard and it wasn't like we were going far.

"Okay, fine," I said and waved goodbye to Serene who was watching us with an odd look on her face. I didn't give it much thought. She was the most unique shifter I'd met so far. I looked for Roman, but he was already gone.

Embry started to jog, and I easily kept up with her as she picked up the pace. "This okay?" she asked.

"Yep, but if you go any faster, I'll let you leave me behind," I replied.

She laughed. "Never."

We were a minute into the run, and she kept glancing at me. "What?" I asked.

"It's just weird. I never expected to share this part of my life with you. Yet, even though you're here, I feel like… I don't know. It's hard to describe, but I know you're not happy. I didn't need to know you in person to know the signs of that truth."

It was getting harder to keep things to myself. Embry wanted me to stay. Roman, too. And I knew there were others who would support my permanent place in the pack, but none of that stopped the twisting ache inside me from growing.

Sure, more than once I'd wished the paranormal worlds I'd read about were real, but wishing and having that become reality were two totally different things. Knowing I was expected to be part of all this was a lot to take in. I was trying to ignore the voice in my head that said to run, but it was harder than I expected.

Though, after speaking with Beatrix, I was nearly certain that if I left, I'd have to fight for my life, and I wasn't ready for that by any means.

"It's not that I'm unhappy, Em. I've only been here a few days, and I'm still trying to decide what I want," I said.

"What if you can't decide?" she asked.

"That's not something to worry about today. I'd prefer to gorge junk food and do nothing like we had planned. Does that work?"

She grinned. "Absolutely."

////

I'd stayed up late the previous night reading while Embry did whatever it was that she did on the computer. Whenever I asked, she went off on a tangent using words I had no desire to understand. She was more of a nerd than I realized when it came to numbers.

I stretched out in bed as the sun beat down on me and groaned. Everything ached, and I blamed it on all the running I did the day before. Apparently, it didn't matter if the action seemed easy; I was still paying for the extra exertion.

Rolling out of my bed, my vision blurred, and I

nearly fell over. "Whoa." I grabbed on to the nightstand, still sitting on the bed, and pushed down the need to vomit. Yeah, this wasn't working.

I stumbled to the door, almost smacking my head on the handle, and ended up crawling to the bathroom.

"Cait?" Embry called out, but I couldn't speak. If I opened my mouth, words weren't going to be what came out.

I made it to the toilet just in time for the retching to begin. My eyes closed as I tried not to think about resting my cheek where people's asses sat, but the cool porcelain felt too good against my heated skin.

"Jesus, Cait. What happened?" She kneeled beside me and pulled my hair back into a ponytail as I started dry-heaving. "Your skin is on fire. Hold on."

Embry disappeared, and I ended up on the tile floor before she got back. I wasn't sure how long she was gone, but she had to shake me awake when she returned.

My eyes focused on her face and saw it was full of concern. "You shouldn't be this sick. Supernaturals don't get sick. Like, none of us."

I wanted to say something witty, but everything hurt, and I only managed to groan. She picked me up from the floor and carried me to my room. "I'm going to get you some ice to suck on," she said.

My head was pounding, and my throat burned from throwing up. I tried sitting up, but even that was too much effort. Embry was back in seconds and saved me the trouble of trying again by shoving two extra pillows behind my head.

"Take this." She held ice to my lips, and as soon as the coolness touched me, I had no problem opening my lips.

"I'm going to call for Ramona. I'm not equipped to handle this," Embry said as I closed my eyes again.

"It's probably just the flu," I mumbled.

"Cait, you're not human anymore. Not really. We can't assume this is just some virus. Not after everything that happened yesterday," she said.

I opened my eyes, a small burst of energy filling me. "Do you think Beatrix made me sick?"

"I hope not, but we can't rule it out. Serene might trust the witch, but we have to consider every possibility." She walked to the door and paused. "I'll be right back. Don't move."

I didn't even have enough strength to nod, so there was a fat chance of me going anywhere. Instead, I closed my eyes and fell back to sleep for who knew how long. When I came around again, I could hear Ramona and Embry talking.

"Do you think it would help even though they're not bonded?" Embry asked.

"Well, it can't hurt. We don't have any idea what we're dealing with. It's really the only option," Ramona replied.

I groaned and tried to roll over. Embry was at my side with a bowl and ice. "Which do you need?"

"Ice," I groaned.

Ramona placed her hand on my leg and swiftly removed it. "She's hotter than a human would be from the flu."

"That's what I thought, too," Embry said.

"What does that mean?" I asked, and they both shared a look. "Tell me."

"Depending on how much your body still thinks it's human, it could start shutting down from the high fever. My estimate is you're hovering around one hundred and five or six degrees right now. Another couple degrees warmer and I'd expect convulsions from a human," Ramona answered.

After everything I'd learned, this was not how I thought I'd be going out.

"I'm going to make her an ice bath," Embry said and darted out of the room.

Ramona sat next to me without touching my skin. "I think having Roman near could help. With bonded mates, when one is injured, being around their other half speeds up the healing process. Being sick isn't something we've ever had to deal with, but I think it would work if you're okay with me bringing him here."

Considering I was close to death, I couldn't tell her no. "Go for it." I'd just have to make sure I kept my clothes on for the bath.

Ramona got up to leave, mentioning it was something to tell him in person rather than telepathically, and Embry was just coming back in. "Tub is filling up and I've dumped all the ice I have in it. Can you bring back more?" Embry asked Ramona.

I didn't hear or see the response. My eyes closed as I grew tired again. Embry picked me up and carried me to the bathroom. "Do you want me to take your pajamas off?"

I shook my head, and she gently placed me in the water. My skin felt like it was sizzling on contact, but it did feel better.

My muscles were easing after a few minutes until I heard a loud bang in the other room. "Where is she?" Roman bellowed before storming into the bathroom.

Our eyes locked and for a moment, I let him in. I accepted his care and concern as he pushed Embry out of the way and kneeled beside me. "Cait."

His hand brushed strands of my hair back, and he gently kissed my forehead. I sighed in relief, letting his name slip from my lips. Ramona had been right. Everything about having him at my side felt good.

"I'm right here, and I'm not going anywhere," he whispered, putting his arm behind my head to help keep me propped up in the water.

"Good," I muttered, accepting what I had no right to. Roman wanted me to be his, and it felt like I was using him when I knew I wanted to be free. Except when I was vulnerable, like when he touched me, I wasn't so sure that was the case, which only made me want my independence more. It was a vicious fucking cycle.

My eyes were closed as I soaked up whatever it was that Roman's presence was offering. More ice was deposited into the tub, but it melted nearly as quickly as it showed up. Ramona and Embry took turns checking in and bringing me water to keep me hydrated.

An hour later, I finally started shivering. "Can I get out yet?" I asked.

"You're still warm, but not like when I arrived. I don't see why not," Roman answered.

His arms lifted me out of the water, and he pressed me against his chest without a second thought.

"I'm getting you wet," I said, as if he couldn't tell.

He frowned at me. "I should be doing that to you."

My eyes widened, and I tried to say something, but no words came out before he winked. "Kidding. Sort of."

I really wanted to punch him, but I didn't have enough energy to do so. "That was rude."

"Yeah, but it was also funny," he said as he sat me on the chair in my room, then went to my dresser.

"Uh, what are you doing?" I asked when he opened a drawer.

"Getting you dry clothes. You don't want to sleep in wet clothes, do you?"

No, I really didn't, but I also didn't want him picking through my underwear.

He already had a sleep shirt and a pair of black boyshorts underwear in hand before I could formulate a proper objection.

Roman's hands reached for my tank top, and I at least had enough strength to grab his hand. "Not going to happen, dude."

He sighed. "You know you can't change yourself right now. I promise not to look."

Something told me Roman was full of shit, but he was once again right. I was barely holding my head up. "Rip the top off and put the shirt on first," I said as my agreement.

"Whatever you want, Kitten," he said, fighting off a grin and using the nickname he'd called me at the cabin.

Both of his hands gripped my top, and he met my eyes. "I'll be watching you the whole time." Then, he tugged, and the fabric began to rip ever so slowly.

Jesus, this was *not* better than him looking.

My chest rose and fell as we locked gazes. My tongue darted out to lick my dry lips, and his eyes followed the movement as he swallowed thickly. My tank top fell at my arms as he let go of it, but neither of us moved for several moments.

"I should put the shirt on now," Roman murmured.

"You should," I replied.

He nodded, reaching for it while never breaking eye contact. My heart raced as he gathered the material and slid it over my head. His hands trailed down my arms to guide my hands through the armholes.

Every touch was like sexual torture.

"Can you stand?" he asked as my body trembled, and I tried to blame the reaction on whatever sickness I had.

I nodded, not trusting my voice. My legs were

wobbly, but I managed to hold on to the arms of the chair as we kept staring at each other.

Roman's hands went underneath my shirt as it fell down to cover my lower half. With one long torturous tug, he slid my shorts and underwear down my legs. I leaned against the chair, practically panting as he pulled them off my feet.

The boyshorts came next, and I wasn't sure how I was going to survive his continued touch. I was ready to combust, and he was having too much fun at my expense.

His fingers skimmed against my skin as he pulled my underwear up under the long shirt.

I tried to look away, but he captured me in his gaze. This was so not good.

Roman grinned when he finished. "Told you I wouldn't look."

I rolled my eyes. "Do you want a treat for being a good boy?"

"I wouldn't say no to one."

Oh, I bet he wouldn't.

I let him help me to the bed, because everything felt like mush, especially after standing those few moments. All from the flu I had.

Yep, totally.

24

ROMAN

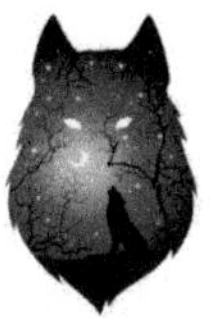

I ended up staying the rest of the night at Embry's cabin. What started as something playful turned into torture for both me and Cait. I'd never wanted someone so badly as I did her when I took her clothes off. If she hadn't been sick, I wasn't sure what would have happened, but damn if I didn't want a repeat as soon as she was better.

Already, her fever was down, but she was exhausted. I could even feel the tug on my own energy as I stayed with her, which I hadn't expected since we weren't bonded. When my mom had come to get me and told me what happened, the sense of panic that took over surprised the hell out of me. I'd already known I was protective of her, but the tear in my chest when I heard the words "Cait is sick" was unlike anything I'd ever experienced.

If anything happened to her, I wasn't sure who I would turn into. I'd only known her a short time. I certainly didn't love her yet, but I already knew I needed Cait in my life.

Embry crept into the room just as I was starting to drift off in the chair I'd moved to the side of the bed. "How's she doing?" Embry whispered.

"Better," I replied.

"Good. Vaughn needs you, so I'll take over," she said.

Panic started to claw at me. If I left, there was a chance Cait's fever would come back.

"Easy there. I'll call for you if it gets worse," Embry added.

"Even the slightest," I said.

She nodded and saluted me. Embry was ridiculous, but she'd been a good friend to Cait. I was grateful my mate had someone like that in her life.

I turned to Cait, brushing her hair back. I didn't want to leave her, but if Vaughn needed me, then it was probably important.

"Why didn't Vaughn call for me himself?" I asked after I realized I hadn't heard from him since I arrived.

"Uh, he didn't want to bother you," Embry said, but I didn't believe her. Something was up.

"Alright. I'll be back as soon as I can. If she wakes up before then, tell her I'm sorry I had to go," I said.

Embry grinned. "She'll be fine, lover boy. Get out of here."

I did as she said, reaching out to Vaughn on my way out the door. *Where are you?*

He replied quickly. Too quickly. *In my office.*

As I headed for the pack house where the office he rarely used was, I saw several pack members. Normally, people waved or at least nodded when I passed by, but most of them just stared this time.

Shit, what had happened?

I tried not to run and draw attention as I hurried to find Vaughn. When I walked in, Collin, one of our top guards and a friend of Sam's, was just coming out of Vaughn's office. "How is Cait?" he asked.

"Better. Thanks," I replied.

"Sam took off. She said you better have your shit figured out before she gets back. She seemed more than pissed she didn't get her normal bestie time in with you while she was home," Collin said.

Damn it. I knew she'd had to go again, but it usually wasn't so soon. She was going to kick my ass when she was home again. Hopefully, she wouldn't be gone for weeks this time around.

"Thanks for letting me know. I'll owe her one."

He nodded. "Sam won't tell you, but she's happy for you. She asked about Cait before she left. We were actually wondering if she's changing into a wolf yet?" he asked.

I raised a brow. "Why would you ask that?"

"We can all sense her energy. It's not like ours, but she's your mate. Just curious," he replied.

He and everyone else. I was going to have to tell the pack something soon. If he was asking, then others would be as well. Only they wouldn't be coming to me.

I nodded and moved past him, fully aware I didn't

answer his question. When I entered Vaughn's office, he was running both hands through his already slicked-back hair.

"Shut the door," he said.

"That bad, huh?" I tried to joke, but he didn't even crack a smile. "What happened?" I sat down, exhausted.

"They thought something happened to you until I convinced them otherwise," he answered.

"What would give them reason to think that?"

"You know the pack all shares energy with you, Roman. Whatever was happening with Cait caused you to pull on the pack. Noticeably."

Shit. I hadn't thought Cait was that bad off. I knew I was helping her, but I'd let her distract me more than I should have. I wasn't paying close enough attention to the impact of my choices. That was a decision that would have ramifications I didn't need.

Vaughn continued, "Some are saying she's a liability and going to make our pack subject to potential takeovers. It doesn't help that Kyle was here yesterday."

Mother fuck. He was right.

"What's been done already?" I asked, because I knew Vaughn wouldn't have just been sitting around.

"I went to the people I knew were known for stirring the shit and might have put a bit of fear in them. Don't worry, I smiled while doing it."

I laughed. "Of course, you did. I'll call a pack meeting for tomorrow. Let me just get through this day.

Cait is already feeling better, so they shouldn't feel any more drain of energy."

"A meeting is a good idea. Stick to facts and have her present. She's a strong woman. Just warn her it might get ugly," Vaughn said, and I hoped like hell he was wrong.

This was the part I'd feared when I found out Cait wasn't a witch screwing with me. People would see her as a weakness I couldn't afford. I'd originally thought the same thing, but the more I got to know her, the more I knew that wouldn't be the case, as long as she stopped fighting what was happening to her.

She had power within her. Potentially a lot of it. The unfortunate part was that I wasn't willing to tell the pack everything yet. Not until we had more facts. I trusted them, but uncertainty made people do stupid shit. I couldn't gamble my mate's wellbeing on the choices others made. Not yet.

My dad knocked at the door, and Vaughn welcomed him in. "How are things?" Dad asked.

"If you're here instead of fishing, then you know exactly how things are," I replied.

He nodded. "I might have heard a thing or two. From your mother and elsewhere."

"I was going to call a pack meeting for tomorrow. What do you think?" I asked him because I would have anyway after leaving Vaughn's office. Dad was alpha for decades. I trusted his opinion when it came to things like this.

"I think it's a good idea, but don't tell them anything

you're not certain about. If anyone asks a question you don't know the answer to, tell them just that. They'll be looking for lies and half-truths, wondering if Cait's appearance in your life will make you choose her over the pack," Dad said.

I grunted. "And what if I would?"

"I know you would, but they don't need to know that. They only need to know that you're still here and protecting them is just as important to you as it was before Cait's arrival. Nothing about that is untrue."

I nodded. He was right about that.

"I need to get back to Cait. I'd like to be there when she wakes up today," I said.

"Are things any better between the two of you?" Dad asked.

I immediately thought about what had happened in her room. "They're getting there."

"Good, but don't let her make you question who you are. If Cait doesn't want to be here, the best thing might be to let her go," Dad said.

Rage filled me in an instant. "How could letting my true mate walk away from me ever be the best thing?"

"Not for you, but for her. She doesn't understand our way of life and thinking. Some time apart might show her what she's missing."

Even if he was right, I couldn't think about that option at the moment. I already knew Cait leaving would break me. My wolves would have a real reason to question my sanity then.

///

I'd tried to hold off having the meeting until Cait was better, but Vaughn convinced me that the longer I waited, the worse things would get. Unfortunately, he'd been right.

Two full days after Kyle had shown up unannounced, half of the pack was ready to throw Cait out. It didn't matter to them that she had a mark from our creator. She was not our equal and more importantly, she was unknown—something that instilled fear into most shifters.

I didn't blame them. My first reaction to Cait had been the same, and I continued to try to remember that, so I didn't become angry with them. I'd once let the fear convince me she would be nothing other than trouble, but the other shifters didn't have a bond to her like I did. Moving past their reservations wasn't going to be an easy thing.

We had nearly one-hundred-fifty members in our pack, including pups, within a thirty-mile radius. When I called the meeting, I expected about a third of them to show up, considering we always recorded the meetings and emailed the videos afterward.

I'd been shown how important Cait's presence was to the shifters when I arrived at the training field. We had no indoor area that was big enough to hold everyone, and there were clusters of shifters standing around when I got there.

"You have your work cut out for you, boss," Vaughn

said, meeting me at the wooden platform he'd helped set up.

"Did you at least warm them up for me?" I asked.

Vaughn nodded. "You know I like my foreplay."

The comment caught me by surprise—even though it really shouldn't have—and I nearly choked from the sudden laughter.

He patted me on the back. "That's better. You needed to lighten up a little. They're going to sense your tension, and that won't help anything."

"Thanks, Vaughn. For everything you've been taking care of since Cait arrived," I said sincerely.

"You know I got your back, bro. Now get up there and calm the masses." Vaughn smacked me on my ass before shoving me forward.

When I stepped onto the stage, I waited until the crowd quieted before speaking, taking the extra few seconds to check on Cait since Embry had stayed home with her.

How are things going? I asked Embry through our wolf connection.

She's fine, lover boy. Still sleeping. Now leave me alone. I'm watching a movie.

Grabbing the microphone from the stand, I cleared my throat. "Thank you all for coming. First, I'd like to apologize for not doing this sooner. I know there have been a lot of questions, and we've tried to answer them individually, but I see now that wasn't the best way to go about our current situation.

"As you all know, when I came back from my

vacation, a new addition arrived at the same time. Her name is Cait Jones. She was born human but has been marked by our creator. Some of you might have heard about the Luna Marked, some not. Either way, we understand how not knowing more about our guest has caused tension within the pack."

"But she's not our guest. She's your mate, right? You have a human mate," Jerome said from the front.

"It is true my wolf has claimed Cait as our mate. It's also true that she *was* human, but the moment she became marked, that ceased to be the case," I said.

"Does she have a wolf then?" he pressed.

"No, but she does have an energy within her that she has been learning to channel. As time goes on, I suspect Cait will be just as strong as us, even if she doesn't have a wolf spirit within her," I answered, hoping they would all focus on the strength portion of my comment.

"Except we don't know for sure. Others will be curious about your mate. What do you plan to do if people start sniffing around? What was Kyle doing here?" Trish asked next.

Those two questions went together, whether I liked it or not, and I knew I was going to have to address them. I'd just hoped to get there on my own instead of being interrogated.

"Kyle was here asking about the Tuttle property. I've denied his request. He did meet Cait, and we told him she was just passing through. He doesn't know what she is, and we hope to keep it that way for the time being. As for others coming around, we have increased the security system around our land here and will be watching for anyone uninvited.

"I would also like to ask that the pack keep their eyes and ears out. Even if you're not tasked with guard duties, we are still family, and Cait's arrival shouldn't change that. I know that the unknown is unnerving, but I promise you that I am doing everything in my power to keep you all safe. That remains a top priority for me."

I scanned the crowd and was met with disapproving frowns. It didn't appear as if I was getting through to any of them. This was not going well.

"How can we expect you to keep us safe when your mate is a liability?" someone from the back yelled, and I didn't catch who it was.

"A group of us are actively working with Cait to ensure she learns how to protect herself, and we are researching the Luna Marked to make sure we understand what her power means for the rest of us," I answered.

"If she's your mate, why is she staying with Embry?" Jerome asked from the front again.

"Cait didn't grow up learning about the meaning of true mates. It's going to take her some time to acclimate to our ways." Jesus, they weren't holding anything back. My private life was on attack, and there wasn't a damned thing I could do about it without upsetting a majority of them.

"And if she never acclimates? What then? We've let a stranger into our home who's learned things about us that she has no right to know. You're putting us all in danger, Roman," Jerome said loudly.

He was going on my list of wolves to keep an eye on. I was all for being transparent, but his questions were bordering on insubordinate.

"This is the last set of questions I will answer. I understand your fears and I respect them, but I am still your alpha. You need to trust that I will make the right choice for the best of the pack. Fate would not have matched me to Cait if she wasn't going to make me a better alpha. Remember who we are, what we come from, and the true meaning behind mates before you judge Cait so harshly. It is not her fault she is in this situation. She did not ask for it, and if you took the time to see things from her perspective, you'd know she was handling all of this amazingly well," I said, pausing before I answered questions I really shouldn't need to.

Nobody else argued with my statements, so I continued, "If you think I haven't thought about Cait rejecting our way of life, then you're wrong. As I said before, I am always considering the pack as a whole. If Cait chooses not to stay here, then we will have her memory wiped. There is no risk of her sharing anything she's learned so far, and wolves will remain safe within our territory."

"And the risk to you?" a different voice yelled from the back.

"As I already stated, I'm not answering any other questions. I need you all to trust me to make the right decision, not only for myself, but the pack as well. If

I've lost your trust, then you're welcome to see me in private to voice any further concerns. For now, the subject is closed. I expect you all to either treat Cait with respect or stay away from her while we figure things out. Even though we're not bonded, she is still my mate and your potential future alpha female.

"When we learn anything in regard to Cait's mark, I will update you all, because I believe that is pertinent information for everyone. Anything outside of what she is capable of is none of anyone's business. If you have any further concerns or questions that don't require immediate action, direct them to my email or to Vaughn and we will handle them as quickly as we can. Thank you all for coming here, and I hope this meeting has helped you understand a little more about my mate." I put the microphone back in its spot and stepped away.

I didn't for one moment believe that the meeting had gone well. I could force my way into their thoughts, but it wasn't necessary. There wasn't a single person who had come to Cait's defense, and that said all I needed to know.

The pack wanted her gone, but that wasn't going to happen. She was mine, and I wasn't letting her go unless she asked.

25

CAIT

Three days passed before I was able to get out of bed. By the time my body didn't feel like it had been run over any longer, I was experiencing full-on cabin fever. Embry, Roman, and Ramona had all taken turns spending time with me, and Serene had checked in twice, but it wasn't the same as leaving the house.

On top of all that, I'd had a near-constant headache, which made reading nonexistent. Being sick was officially my least favorite thing.

I walked out of my bedroom, freshly showered and feeling human with no fever and only minor aches. Embry was grabbing her bag from the hook, and I practically attacked her.

My hands wrapped around her shoulders, and I spun her toward me. "Where are you going?"

She didn't seem the least bit fazed. "To work. You're supposed to be in bed. I only let you take a shower because I was beginning to smell you from the living room."

I sighed. Heavily. "Feel my head. The fever is gone. I need to get out of here. If you don't take me with you, then I'll just leave when you're gone."

Embry peeled my fingers away. "You're a pain in my ass."

"But you love me anyway, so you're not going to make this harder than it needs to be." I grinned, because I knew she had no argument. I might not be back to normal, but was there even such a thing as normal anymore? I didn't think so.

"Fine, but I need to tell you something," she said, shifting her feet while avoiding eye contact.

I shook my head. "Not now, please. Just give me this one day before everything goes back to weird wolfy things. I just want one regular day."

After spending so much time with myself, I knew that I had to reevaluate my thinking. Yes, I wanted my freedom and free will, but Beatrix had made me think a little harder about how I needed to go about things.

Just because I was in the pack didn't mean I had to have a bond with Roman. I was smart enough to realize that the only way I could be safe back out in the world was if I stuck around long enough to get myself under control.

Serene had mentioned having me come by when I was feeling better so we could work together again. With as old as she was and the fact that she was the historian, I didn't think it would be smart to turn her down.

Today, I wanted as much normalcy as I could get. Then, first thing tomorrow, I'd be going to Serene's while Embry worked. Even though I'd have preferred my best friend to be the one training me, she had an important role in the pack herself. I didn't want to be a distraction to her.

Embry seemed hesitant to keep her thoughts to herself. "Is what you want to say life or death?" I asked.

"Not that I'm aware of," she replied.

"Then, it can wait." My eyes pleaded with her to agree.

She grabbed my hand. "I repeat, you're a pain in my ass."

I didn't bother to reply. I knew she was right, but she also knew I needed this. Hopefully, after she was done doing whatever was required in the office, we'd be able to go do something fun. Maybe go out to dinner or something human. I needed that more than anything.

We got in the jeep, and I enjoyed the sunshine soaking into my skin as she drove the short distance to the mill. My eyes closed as hair whipped around my face, and I let my hand bounce around in the wind. As we slowed down, I tamed my strands and took in the mill.

It was busier than the last time we'd been there. More trucks were waiting for loads of supplies, and people, most likely shifters, moved about like a well-oiled machine. Embry guided me into the main store entrance, and we headed straight to her office, which was already remodeled.

Vaughn sat with his feet on top of his new metal desk. "About time you showed your face around here. I was going to recommend you be relieved of duties."

The room was a soft yellow like I'd previously suggested with a black silhouette painting covering the whole left side of the room. A large moon took up the center with trees all around and wolves placed casually along rolling hills. It didn't seem unnatural or call attention to anything supernatural.

Embry grunted. "You touched my stuff."

"You weren't here to move it yourself, and I warned you I was changing things up," Vaughn replied, dropping his feet to the floor and getting up.

"Yeah, well, I was a little busy," Embry huffed. Busy because of me, but I didn't feel too bad. It wasn't as if she hadn't been able to work while I was sick.

Vaughn stalked toward me, a grin on his face. "You're causing all sorts—"

A stapler came an inch from breaking Vaughn's nose, and he turned toward Embry as he caught it. "*That* won't go unpunished."

Embry laughed, but it sounded forced. "Get over it."

Vaughn nodded and sat back down. "I guess I'll just sit here and look pretty. You're lucky it's not a hardship on my behalf."

I chuckled, and Embry glared at me, but I ignored her. I liked Vaughn. He kept things light and fun and made me forget all the shit going on. I wished Embry was attracted to him. I could see them being good together.

Embry sorted through the papers I assumed Vaughn had left on her desk. She used a red pen and marked all over them, mumbling words I was probably better not hearing. Vaughn's smile, on the other hand, got bigger the more she grumbled.

"Want to play tic-tac-toe?" Vaughn asked me.

"Sure," I replied, moving my chair to his desk.

"Traitor," Embry complained, but I was bored and didn't care.

We played too many rounds to count before Embry was done. I kicked his ass the first half-dozen games until he figured out my trick, and the rest of the rounds ended in a tie.

"I need Vaughn to show me one of the loads that isn't right. We'll be gone maybe ten minutes. Don't leave this room. Do you understand?" Embry said, her face creased with worry.

"I think I can manage to keep myself entertained for that long," I replied, not understanding why she was so tense.

"Good." She smacked Vaughn on the back of the head. "Let's go."

The two of them left, and I began to doodle on the paper we'd been using for the child's game. Too bad I hadn't thought to bring my phone. I never was able to finish the book that had finally started getting good.

Vaughn had left the door cracked when they went out the back and the saws were going. I tried to ignore the sound, but it was grating on my nerves after a couple minutes. When I closed the door, the noise became a dull roar.

Poking around the room, I didn't find anything interesting, and only another minute had passed. I leaned back in Embry's chair, staring at the ceiling until I couldn't take it anymore.

When I glanced at the clock, it had only been four minutes since Embry and Vaughn disappeared. I'd been cooped up in my room for too long, and the need to be outside was driving me nearly crazy.

I peeked out the back door and didn't see anyone. Given I knew nothing about the mill, I decided to wait out front instead, then scribbled a note to them and left it on Embry's desk.

Going into the store front, I noticed Chloe, the cashier from before, was stocking shelves. I snuck past her and slid quietly out the front door.

A breeze brushed against my skin, and I sighed. "This is so much better."

Embry's jeep wasn't locked, so I headed there. I didn't want to freak her out by leaving the parking lot. The sun was out, but with the wind, the heat wasn't as unbearable as it had been the first few days I'd been here.

Closing my eyes, I leaned my head back on the seat and took in the sounds and smells around me. The heady scent of freshly cut wood was the most prominent, and I inhaled greedily.

Just as I relaxed, I heard something snap. My eyes

shot open, and I was jumping out of the jeep without a second thought. A few of the mill workers were gathered around a truck that seemed to be dropping off fresh logs, and one of the straps holding the load broke.

I could see the second and third about to give from where I stood. The guys below it had no idea. They were going to get squished in a matter of seconds. Damn it. I couldn't just stand there and do nothing.

"Watch out!" I yelled as I ran toward them, but nobody was paying attention.

Another tie-down broke. This time, they must have heard it as well. Two of the three men were already moving out of the way, but a third seemed to think he could fix whatever disaster was about to happen by messing with the remaining straps.

Without thinking, I jerked on his arm. "You have to move," I yelled, but he was twice my size and didn't budge.

"Don't touch me," the guy barked at the same time I heard the wood start to tumble.

His dark eyes glared at me with a malice that didn't make any sense to me considering I didn't know who he was. He was wearing a mill polo, so I at least knew he was a shifter and should probably be more careful, but I didn't have time to be cautious.

"I'm not sorry for this," I said as I channeled my energy and used the extra strength to shove him out of the way at just the right moment.

He stumbled, and I followed after, keeping upright as we ran to get out of the way. Nobody else was near us as the first logs began to fall. I heard them splinter as I kept moving toward the safety of the fence, but I didn't quite make it there.

One of the logs was quicker than I was. It was a smaller one, maybe four inches around, and most likely one from the top, but it still hurt like hell when I crashed to the ground, bracing myself with my arms while the log rolled over me.

At first, I thought I was fine—bruised and scratched all over, but nothing time wouldn't heal. Then, I tried to kick the log off of me only to have a sharp pain race through me before realizing I was bleeding. No, not just oozing crimson. There was also a splinter of what I assumed to be bone poking through my skin at my ankle.

My panic levels rose as I tried not to lose my shit. I heard my name screamed but couldn't stop staring at my foot.

The man I'd saved stood over me without a scratch to be seen. Of course, he hadn't gotten hurt.

"You saved me," he muttered.

"Duh. Care to help?" I snapped, a fury rolling through me from the pain moving up my leg.

"Jerome, are you okay?" one of the other men asked.

He nodded as he threw the log off of me. Before I could try and get up, Vaughn and Embry were at my side. Each of them had tense jaws and angry eyes.

"What the hell happened?" Vaughn asked as he cradled my head in his hands.

I quickly rattled off my version, and by the time I

was done, I could barely breathe from the pain moving through my body.

My head wobbled when I made the mistake of looking down again. "That's really not good."

Vaughn lifted my chin. "Best not to look, sweetheart."

Embry pinched the bridge of her nose. "You couldn't have just stayed in the office? Roman is going to kill us." She turned to Vaughn. "Carry her to the jeep. We need to get back to the pack."

"Uh, pretty sure I need a hospital, Em," I said, then screamed as Vaughn pressed on my ankle. "What the hell, dude?"

"Sorry, I had to, uh, push the bone back in so it didn't snag on anything."

Tears fell freely from my eyes while I tried to breathe through the pain. When that didn't work, I closed my eyes and imagined sitting on the beach in Australia with nobody else around.

Embry settled her hand on my shoulder. "There's a doctor already headed to the house, one whose family has helped our pack on the rare occasions we need it. Normally, it's for blood or materials, but I'm sure broken bones aren't a problem for him, either."

"Okay, let's go then," I said through clenched teeth.

There wasn't a graceful way to get me in the jeep, and there was no keeping the tears at bay as Vaughn launched himself into the back seat. He settled me into the seat, then lifted my leg until my foot rested in his lap. I refused to look at it again as I did my best to ignore the sensations pulsing in my foot. Finally, a numbness began to set in and it didn't hurt as bad as it had just five minutes before.

Embry carefully drove out of the parking lot before picking up speed on the main road. I focused on the back of the headrest to keep from looking at the blood I knew was getting all over Vaughn. But then, he jostled my leg and I howled in pain. Maybe it wasn't numbness I was sensing before.

"You have zero bedside manner," I grumbled, my gaze going to his face and finding his shirt halfway off.

"Calm down. That likely scared you more than it hurt. You're getting blood all over my favorite jeans. Shirt is already ruined, so might as well try to staunch the flow of crimson before a vamp shows up," he replied, keeping his face serious.

My jaw dropped, and Embry groaned. "Not something to joke about with her, Vaughn."

He shrugged. "I thought it was funny."

If I thought I could do it without further hurting myself, I'd have kicked him. Instead, we pulled into the pack driveway, and I hoped like hell the doctor was already there. Though, as Vaughn wrapped my foot, it didn't hurt nearly as much as I expected it to, considering the glimpse of gore I'd gotten earlier. My pain receptors didn't seem to know what they wanted to do.

"What happened?" Roman demanded before we'd fully come to a stop.

"One of the drivers had shitty straps. They started to break, and Cait saved Jerome from being made into a pancake, sacrificing her safety in the process. She likely saved his life and earned herself a broken ankle," Vaughn said loudly, and I assumed for the benefit of those around us. Though, he was exaggerating some and I didn't know why. I doubted the logs would have killed a wolf shifter. Just banged them up more than they would have liked.

Voices began to murmur, and Embry added, "I saw the whole thing as we were running to help. Cait ran toward the danger and did whatever she could to help even when her verbal warnings were being ignored."

Roman stepped in to separate me from everyone else as the crowd drew closer. Something had happened, and I wanted to know what.

"For those of you ready to run off and share what you learned here today, make sure your story is right. If I hear anything other than what Vaughn and Embry have said, you'll be seeing me shortly after," Roman said, and the other shifters began to disperse quietly.

Another car pulled in behind us, and an older gentleman got out of the black sedan with a large medical bag.

"Get her to the empty office so Dr. Sanders can examine her foot," Roman said to Vaughn before walking to greet the new arrival.

"Sorry if this hurts," Vaughn said as he moved to get us out of the jeep.

I braced for the pain, but it never came. There was

plenty of discomfort, but nothing like when I'd gotten into the jeep.

"Damn, Cait. You're one tough chick. I expected a lot more tears out of you," Vaughn said as he carried me into the house.

Embry smiled next to us. "That's my bestie. I know an awesome person when I see one."

"Or in our case, when you read their comments," I joked, because we'd been friends for months before we first video chatted.

Vaughn took me into an empty office and sat me on top of the desk. "Sorry, we don't have something more comfortable. It's not too often people get hurt bad enough around here that we need a special room for them," he said.

I shrugged, not really knowing how to respond. I wasn't uncomfortable any longer, and I was pretty sure that wasn't normal.

Roman and Dr. Sanders came in a moment later. The doctor came straight to me. "Did you hit your head when this happened?"

"No, but I did get dizzy afterward. Though, that was probably from all the blood," I said.

Roman growled from next to me, his arm coming around my shoulders as the doctor unwrapped my foot.

I turned away so I didn't get nauseous again but regretted it as my eyes locked on Roman's. His gaze was intense, and my heart picked up speed as I tried to decide which was worse: being so close to him again or having my foot shattered from a load of lumber.

"Well, that's interesting," the doc murmured, catching everyone's attention.

"What is?" Embry asked first.

He poked at my foot. "She should be at least wincing when I do that if she had broken bones in there. I can't even find where all of this blood came from."

Roman left my side and joined the doctor. As they both inspected me, I felt tender spots, but nothing horrendous.

"Unbelievable. Not even a full shifter should have healed that fast," Roman said in awe.

"Can you wiggle your toes?" the doctor asked.

I concentrated more than necessary. They moved without issue or pain.

The doctor gathered his things, quick to get out of there. "Well, it seems my services aren't needed. I'll show myself out."

Vaughn moved to follow Dr. Sanders anyway, leaving me alone with Roman and Embry.

Roman moved my ankle around slowly. "How does that feel?"

"It's sore, but nothing like it was," I said, then remembered something. "I had to use my power to push that guy out of the way. Do you think that helped heal me?"

"It's the only logical explanation. It should have taken a shifter a couple of days to get to this point," Roman answered.

"How did Cait end up alone out front?" Roman

demanded, reminding me that Embry had been awfully shady about things beforehand.

"She doesn't listen well, that's how. We only left her alone for like five minutes," Embry said.

I pointed at both of them. "The two of you are hiding something. There should have been no reason why I couldn't be alone outside the office, so start talking. Now."

Embry smirked at him. "I tried to warn you that she'd be after balls if you tried to hide this from her."

I raised a brow. "Given that you knew and didn't tell me straight away, I'm after your tits, too. Tell me what I missed while I was sick."

"Hey, that's not fair. I tried to tell you this morning," Embry replied and I nodded. She was right and I shouldn't have been so adamant about having a "normal" day. Those just didn't exist anymore.

Roman sighed. "Let's go to my office."

"Gladly," I said as I slid off the table gently. Even though I should have washed the dried blood off my foot first, it was time for answers and full disclosure from everyone.

Including me.

26

ROMAN

Something told me I was going to regret having this conversation at that very moment, but Cait had been on pack lands for more than a week. She knew what she was to me. She knew she was no longer human.

It was time to lay things out in a more direct way.

I might have been all for claiming Cait, but I've been trying to see things from her perspective and I'm worried, my wolf said as I walked down the hallway to my office.

I am, too. She knows what she wants already. I can see it in her eyes.

And what if it's not what you want? What we want? he asked, already sounding defeated, which didn't bode well for my confidence.

Then, we'll deal with it, I said, ending the conversation.

I wasn't a patient man. I was an alpha, and when

things needed to be done, I got them done. At some point, I needed to take my emotions out of this situation. Otherwise, I was going to fail at more than I was prepared for.

The three of us silently went up the stairs to my office. With every step, the tension increased. I wished it was just me and Cait having this conversation, but I knew Embry was a big part of things as well.

"Listen, Cait. You have to understand that things work differently around here," Embry started as I shut the door.

"I do understand, but it doesn't mean I'm just going to fall in line with whatever you guys say. I know I can't go back to the life I had, but I also don't want one forced on me, either," she said, and I knew she meant the mate bond.

"Have I forced anything on you?" I asked as I moved to stand behind my desk.

She sighed. "No, but I'm well aware that there are certain expectations of me, and I don't like that. I just want to be me."

"We don't have any expectations. We just want you to be safe," Embry replied.

Cait narrowed her gaze at her. "Really? You don't hope that I'm going to stay here forever, mate with your alpha, and become whatever this mark means?" Cait waved her wrist for emphasis as her voice rose.

Embry wasn't one to back down from anyone. While I might have thought Cait would be an exception to that, I was wrong.

She got in Cait's face. "Of course I hope for all of those things, but that doesn't mean I expect them. You're my best friend. I won't apologize for wanting to keep you in my life. Nor will I be sorry for doing whatever it takes to keep you safe. You don't know anything about this world, but I'm trying to teach you. Can't you see that?"

Cait's stance softened as some of the fight left her eyes. "I'm sorry, Em. It's just been a long few days."

"It has been for all of us. I just hope you'll remember we're on your side," Embry said before turning for the door. "I'm going to go check on things with the pack. There's going to be talk, and we'll want to stay ahead of it."

Embry slipped out the door, closing it behind her before either of us could object. Sure, I'd wanted to have this conversation with Cait alone at first, but since it had turned in a negative direction already, I wished Embry had stayed.

Cait settled into the chair in front of my desk, and I took my own seat. "I'm sorry we didn't tell you everything as it was happening, but I was handling the pack," I said.

"And what happened with the pack that affects me so much?" she asked.

At this point, honesty was the only way to go, so I held nothing back. "Some of them aren't happy you're here. They think you'll make me weak and bring trouble to our lands. I told them that wasn't the case and that they either needed to be nice to you or keep their distance."

She raised a brow. "I don't imagine they took that very well."

"They took it just fine. I'm their alpha. While they're not forced to stay here, they know if they do there are rules to follow. If I ask something of them, it's expected they'll listen or leave," I said.

"What about me? Are you going to ask something of me, then tell me to leave if I don't agree?" she asked, the challenge clear in her bright eyes.

I placed both of my hands on the desk and took a deep breath. "Cait, I've made it very clear that I accept you as my mate. I know this is a weird concept for you, but a bond is something special. The purest form of magic for our kind. I found you attractive the moment I laid eyes on you, even when I thought the pull toward you was fabricated. That is enough for me to want to move forward with whatever is between us.

"I never wanted to pressure you, but you're a grown woman. Deep down, you already know what you want, and I don't need to be coddled. If you don't want to be here, if you don't want me, just say the word. We'll find somewhere else for you to be until you can sort out what the mark means for you," I said, even though each word was like a new knife being plunged into my heart.

My wolf whimpered inside at my words, but he voiced no objections. Something with him had changed. He either knew something or had plans he wasn't sharing. I wasn't sure how okay I was with that, but it wasn't a problem I could focus on then.

Cait's mouth slipped open in surprise. She hadn't expected me to give her an out. Good. Keeping her on her toes wasn't a bad thing.

Tears filled her eyes, but none fell as she straightened her stance and put on a brave face. "Roman, I can't be your mate. My mind and heart don't work like yours. I'm not okay with having my future chosen for me."

It was one thing to expect her rejection and a whole other to hear it. My heart slowed as agony took over. My muscles tensed, and I moved my hands beneath the desk, afraid I'd break something and frighten her. Words failed to come out as I roared on the inside.

This can't be happening, I thought.

Trust that if she is really meant to be ours, then she will be, my wolf said, and I snarled at him.

I didn't want to hear his acceptance. I needed him to rage with me.

What do you know? I asked him.

I'm trusting my instincts. I wouldn't keep something important from you that had to do with Cait. I promise.

He was all I had in that moment to keep me from losing my shit in front of Cait. I settled on trusting him like I always had.

"If you want me to leave the pack, then I will, but I'd like to stay for now. I know that's selfish of me to ask, but I trust you and Embry," Cait said softly.

"But you don't want me," I replied stiffly.

"I'm sorry, Roman," she said, this time meeting my burning gaze. She didn't answer my question. She couldn't without lying. I knew a part of her wanted me. It just wasn't enough. Her rejection told me that I wasn't enough.

I stood up, the chair slamming into the wall from my added force. "I don't need your pity, Cait. I was fine before you came here, I'll be fine while you sort your shit out, and I'll be fine when you leave. Do whatever it is that you'd like. I won't get in your way."

I knew I should have been more careful with my words. There had to be a chance I could still win her over, but the fury storming within me didn't allow for niceties. At least, not yet. Maybe one day.

She stood to follow me as I headed toward the door, but I held my hand up. "We're done here. I'll send Embry or my mother to find you. They'll be your points of contact within the pack now. You can trust Ramona, and she'll help you with Serene. If you want to choose your own destiny, then working with them is the best way to do that."

"Roman, I—"

I couldn't stop the rumble from leaving my chest. She was going to say something she didn't mean because she felt bad, and I didn't need that.

"Clean break, Cait. I'm an all-in kind of person. I would have given you all the time you needed, but you made your point clear. We are not going to be mates. The pull we have will fade over time, and that will be that. I'll keep my distance to make things easier for you, and I ask that you do the same for me."

Tears finally fell from her eyes, and I wanted nothing more than to wrap her in my arms, but she wasn't mine. Not like I hoped she would be.

Cait had made her choice, one I'd known was a possibility all along, but I'd also hoped that the moments we'd had together meant something.

Clearly, that wasn't the case. She was now going to see the alpha side of me. The one that showed very little emotion.

I turned away from her, leaving her alone in my office and using every bit of my resolve to ignore the sounds of her cries. They weren't mine to make better. I wouldn't give Cait any part of me if she didn't want all of me.

I reached out to Embry, letting her know Cait and I were done and that she needed to come get her friend before cutting off the connection. She wasn't getting any other information out of me. Just what she needed to be there for Cait.

Let's run, my wolf said.

Gladly, I replied.

As soon as we stepped outside, I sprinted for the trees and lunged into my shift, taking the small satisfaction at the sound of my clothes shredding.

If I was going to survive this rejection, I needed the freedom and simplicity my wolf's mind provided. I didn't know how long we'd be on our run and didn't care, as long as every step forward dulled the pain currently crushing my heart.

It's going to take time, my wolf added.

I took control and howled out my fury instead of answering him. There was a burn tearing through my soul as we raced through our property. He was wrong. Time had nothing to do with this. Strength was all we needed.

Strength to walk away from Cait and give her the distance we would both need.

If I was a lesser alpha, I'd have taken what I wanted and forced her to be mine, but that wasn't who I was. I never would be the monster who could do that.

I'd accept the pain and find a way to channel it into something else, something that would keep me moving forward instead of crumbling. Distance was what we needed. I had to stay away until the drive to claim Cait wasn't choking me.

The only problem was that with every bound and leap my wolf took away from our mate, the need to turn back to her grew more demanding.

27

CAIT

I hadn't expected things to go so badly, to get so emotional. My heart cracked when I said I couldn't be Roman's mate. Then, as he spoke with so much hurt laced into his voice, the crack formed into fissures I wasn't sure would ever be healed. Only I didn't know if that was the truth or just what the magic forcing me to want Roman was telling me.

That was the shittiest part of all.

I didn't know enough about this world to know truth from lie, reality from magic. Maybe in a way, there was a truth to my feelings for Roman, but I knew myself. If I accepted him now, I'd always question our relationship. There would be resentment, and that wasn't fair to either of us.

My happily-ever-after didn't include fabricated love. No, I wanted something real and tangible and natural.

At least, that's what I kept telling myself as tears spilled down my cheeks.

Roman had walked away from me, leaving me alone in his office. I tried to follow, but he didn't want me near him and it seemed so easy for him to walk away.

Okay, that was a lie. Nothing about this was "easy" for either of us. I could at least accept that, and I'd respect Roman's wishes. He wanted a clean break, and I'd give him one.

Embry rushed through the door, and I was in her arms before I could say a word.

"I'm so sorry, Cait. I never wanted any of this for you. Not like this," she murmured into my hair.

"I know. Let's just go back to your place. Give me tonight to let my emotions do whatever they will. Tomorrow, I'll put forth serious effort into figuring out whatever is inside me," I said.

She led me out the door, and I was thankful there was nobody lingering in our path. "I'm going to tell Vaughn I'm off for the next few days. We're going to figure this out together. I promise," Embry said with conviction.

I just hoped when we did figure out what exactly I was, things weren't worse than I was already picturing.

///

THE FOLLOWING MORNING, I WAS UP AT SUNRISE. EMBRY had already set things up with Serene and Ramona, and I was eager to get started.

I'd cried and yelled and laughed over and over again the night before. I'd had a lot to get off my chest, and Embry accepted all of my mixed emotions without ever once telling me how to feel or making me feel bad for the choices I'd made.

That was why I loved her so much. She respected me as my own person, not for what I could do for her or anything else.

Embry was up and dressed before me, waiting by the door with two steaming mugs. "I thought a heavy dose of caffeine would be helpful before we got started."

"You know the sign above your door is a total lie. I haven't seen you sleep in once since I arrived," I teased as I accepted the drink.

She shrugged. "I don't need much sleep. I just don't like to *people* before noon if I don't have to. Don't tell anyone." She winked, then turned serious. "You know they're not going to take it easy on you today, right?"

I grimaced. "I know."

We went outside to the UTV. The air was sticky and already nearing warm, which told me today was going to be a scorcher.

Embry drove to Serene's house, and we arrived to find Ramona shifting from wolf to human. I'd caught a glimpse of her light tan wolf and was surprised by how much smaller it seemed compared to Roman's.

Then, I shook my head. I couldn't already be thinking about him. I'd done enough of that the night before. Today was for me and me only.

"Good morning, ladies," Ramona said as she ran her fingers through her short hair.

"The sun isn't even all the way up. I wouldn't call the morning good just yet," Embry said, and I had to agree with her, but I was excited either way.

Serene's front door creaked open, and she poked her head out. "Are you three going to stay outside, or can we get the torture started?"

I gulped when she said torture, but I also knew Serene was a little nutty with her choice of words and tried not to let it bother me.

Embry guided me into the house, and I took a seat in the first empty chair at the table to my left. "So, what's first?" I asked.

Serene tapped her forehead. "Meditation. If your mind isn't clear, your energy isn't either." She walked into the living area to our right and sat on the floor. "Come, dear."

It wasn't like I didn't already know this part from working with Embry, but I indulged her anyway.

Embry and Ramona joined me as we all headed to sit with Serene. She patted the spot in front of her. "Right here."

I did as she said, and the others flanked us. Closing my eyes, I focused on breathing, but every time I tried to clear images from my mind, Roman's face appeared.

A hard smack hit me dead center on my forehead. "The hell?"

Serene sneered at me. "Focus."

"Yeah, I'm trying," I snapped.

"You will never be able to protect yourself if you let

human emotions prevent you from being your true self," Serene said.

"Really? And what is my true self?" I asked with bite.

Serene grinned. "I might know something, but it's not my job to tell you. Neither is it Beatrix's, or Embry's, or anyone's. This is for you to figure out. I stand by my previous statement that you need to come to me with answers and not questions. Anyone around you is merely here to guide you. The choices you make are still up to you."

Her words hit me in the gut. They were everything I'd said I wanted, but at the same time felt wrong now. It didn't matter, though. I had made my decision, and I was going to deal with the repercussions.

"You can do this, Cait," Embry encouraged.

I tried again, this time focusing on the end game of all this: my freedom.

The more I meditated, the more I realized that it wasn't about clearing my mind—at least not for me. I had to picture what I wanted most and make it a reality. Only then was I able to feel the energy within me grow in strength.

"That's it. Hold on to that feeling you have right now. Memorize the strength and find a way to recall the power you're channeling by instinct instead of thought. Until you can find a way to be this version of yourself all of the time, you aren't prepared for what's beyond the pack borders," Serene said.

My skin pulsed everywhere, but more so where I

knew the mark to be. I kept my eyes closed as I tried to identify the sensations and burn them into my memory.

When I felt my temperature rising, I shut everything down and opened my eyes. "Is everyone okay?"

Embry and Ramona were grinning while Serene frowned. "How did you do that?" she asked me.

"Do what?"

She waved her hands around me. "Shut it all off like that. As soon as you began to spiral, the energy disappeared."

"I didn't want to hurt anyone. I've been practicing and can tell when I'm getting too hot," I replied.

Serene hummed as she stood to walk away. I turned to the others. "Did I do something wrong?"

"No, you did everything right, and Serene bet it would take all day," Embry answered.

Well, that didn't make sense. "She let me practice in her house when she hoped I'd fail? I could have burned the place down."

Ramona shook her head. "Beatrix didn't sense any fire within you. We don't believe the scorch marks we saw were what we thought. Your energy is powerful and isn't getting used the way it should. You can't shift. You're not releasing it freely. So, when it has the chance to escape, the power wants to run hot and fast."

"So, it's like friction burns from the molecules inside me?" I asked.

Embry coughed. "Nerd."

Whatever. Science was one of the classes I enjoyed

most. It was nice to have a human concept to compare the magic within me to.

"We believe so," Ramona continued. "Our hope is that the more you use the energy, the more you're able to channel without thought, that it will calm down and not seem daunting. Once you can do that, we can move on to defensive tactics."

"That sounds easy enough. I'll work on managing the power inside and let you guys know when I stop heating up." I moved to get up, thinking I could do the rest of the training on my own.

Embry laughed. "Where do you think you're going?"

"Uh, outside?"

Serene rejoined us and threw a bottle at me. "Drink that. Then we go again."

"What is it?" I asked.

"Herbal tea," she replied too quickly.

I didn't believe her for one second, but I also didn't think she was poisoning me. I opened the container and gulped down as much as I could without smelling or tasting the liquid. That only lasted for a few seconds before I began to gag.

"Seriously. What is that?" I asked as I wiped a palm over my mouth.

"A little peppermint, chamomile, ashwagandha, cannabidiol, and a few family secrets you'll never get out of my head," Serene answered.

That last one made it sound as if I was going to start craving the taste of humans, and I tried not to freak out.

Serene took the bottle from me. "Each day you begin training, you'll need to take a few swigs of this. It will help you focus until you're capable of doing so on your own."

Note to self: figure this shit out if only so I never have to taste that crap again.

"Right. I'll be sure not to forget." Even as I said the words, I felt the normal buzz of my mind quieting. Maybe she wasn't so nutty after all.

"Now, let's go outside and draw on the energy around us," Serene said, heading out the front door.

I glanced at Ramona and Embry. "Are you guys sure she's the best person to be helping me?"

"Serene isn't the strongest wolf, but she's our most knowledgeable pack member. Until you're ready for self-defense, she's your best bet," Ramona answered.

Embry swung her arm around me. "But don't worry. We'll be here every step of the way."

28

CAIT

For the first few days, I was positive my freedom was within grasp and I was going to be able to give fate the middle finger. I'd begun to channel more of my energy during the day without having to be solely focused on it.

Every time I succeeded, I grew stronger. The only thing that gnawed at me was that I hadn't seen Roman once since our discussion in his office. Embry and Ramona hadn't brought him up, either, and I'd managed to avoid the rest of the pack since the mill incident.

After I'd learned the pack wanted me gone, I went out of my way to keep to myself. I didn't want to be where I wasn't wanted, and if Roman was so easily able to keep his distance, he hadn't been all that attached to begin with. At least, that was what I kept telling myself.

Today was supposed to be the first day I began defensive training. Even though Serene wouldn't be directly involved in this part, I still expected to see her when we arrived at the field, but instead, it was only Ramona.

"Cait. Embry." She smiled at both of us.

"Where's Serene?" I asked.

"She had some things to do today, but she'll join us tomorrow. No reason we can't continue without her," Ramona answered. I was glad she hadn't made things awkward between the two of us and my reservations had been unfounded.

As I tried to channel my energy, Embry jumped on me. My reflexes were slower than I'd grown used to over the last couple days, but I at least didn't crash to the ground.

"Focus, Cait. That was too slow," Ramona snapped as I backed up.

I'd never been much for physical exercise, and I was really regretting that decision. Embry had tried teaching me some simple moves that seemed easy in the beginning, but with one hit today, my body was sore and sluggish.

"Maybe it's too soon," Embry said as she circled me, bouncing on the balls of her feet.

I shook my head. "No, I'm fine. Go again."

Embry frowned, but she listened to me. I braced myself and recalled her previous instructions. Balance my weight, focus on where my attacker's feet were, and remember to breathe.

The words were easy to understand, but not so easy

to complete when someone was launching themselves at me, ready to strike.

Embry hit me again. This time, I went straight to my ass on the ground. She was my best friend, someone I could trust. It was hard to believe she was really trying to hurt me, and I wondered if that was why I couldn't channel the energy to defend myself.

She helped me up, and I sighed. "Sorry. Maybe you're right."

Ramona stepped closer. "This might be a side effect of…" Instead of finishing, Ramona shared a look with Embry.

I had a feeling I knew what Ramona wanted to say and was grateful she hadn't. I needed to be able to do this without Roman. Clean break. It was what he needed, and I wouldn't be so heartless to drag him back when nothing had changed.

Which seemed stupid as hell. I knew what I was giving up. The chance at an epic love. A family. A safe place with a man who wanted me. To be around my best friend every day. Nothing should compare to those things.

Except I couldn't get out of my own head.

Roman had taken one look at me and "knew" I was his. Something within him—a magical power—told him I was his perfect match. Yet what if I wasn't? What if he got to know me, then decided the fact I wasn't a wolf shifter was too much to handle? Fear and lack of control were causing self-doubt that wasn't easy to move beyond.

If someone could accept a mate so easily, they could also dismiss them just as quickly. I had to know I was capable of taking care of myself before I made any other decisions, and that meant denying him even if I wasn't sure that was the right choice.

Maybe the future would bring different choices, but for now, I was on my own.

Well, with Embry and I guessed Ramona and Serene, too.

Embry and Ramona were hissing at each other as I had my self-reflection, but I was done with being babied.

"That's enough. I'm not a delicate flower. You can say his name around me. I know he still exists."

"He's been gone since that day, you know?" Embry said.

My eyes widened. "Roman left the pack?"

Ramona nodded. "He's supposed to be back today. He just needed time."

Huh. Well, good for him for taking it.

"You think the fact we've been apart is making me weaker?" I asked.

Ramona brushed her hair back and twisted her hands together. "Possibly. I'd like to think we're not that dependent on our mates, but given that the two of you never bonded, you're in a weird place most wolves don't have to deal with."

"Sounds a lot like the mark as well," I mumbled.

Embry nudged me with her hip. "I know it might feel like we're not getting anywhere, but it's only been two weeks since you got that mark. Don't be hard on yourself and rush things."

"I need to, though. It's not like I'm welcome here. I know why we practice all the way out here. Why Serene is the only one helping. I can't stay here for long," I said.

Ramona smiled, the complete opposite of what I'd thought she'd do. "Do you remember the man you saved?"

I nodded. How could I forget? He'd nearly gotten himself killed because he didn't want to listen to me.

"Well, he was one of the ones complaining most about you. He's not your fan now, by any means, but he has quieted. Plus, the pack is like high school with their gossip. Everyone knows what you did. That you risked your life for one of their own. That changes things for a lot of them," Ramona said.

"Then why do I feel like you guys have been hiding me?" I asked.

Embry grimaced. "I thought it would make you feel more comfortable. I should have asked."

I waved a hand. "It's whatever. I'm just glad they don't all hate me."

"Nobody could ever hate you, Cait," Embry said.

Ha. I bet Roman did.

"How about we take the day off? You've been working nonstop since the accident. You might have healed quickly, but rest is just as important. There will be a barbecue later as well. You guys can come check that out if you're up, or stay at Embry's," Ramona said, and I agreed with parts of her suggestion.

"Can we go to town? Eat dinner there and walk around?" I asked, remembering I hadn't gotten to do that before.

Embry smiled. "You know it. Let's shower and change, then head out. We can make a day of it, then get to bed early."

I turned to Ramona. "Do you want to come and skip the other stuff?"

"As fun as that sounds, the two of you enjoy yourselves. I'd like to be here when Roman gets back," she answered.

I left it at that, not wanting to say much more about him. Instead, I focused on getting in a day of normal human activities.

It was about damned time.

///

THE DAY WAS A BUST. I'D THOUGHT CHECKING OUT A small town would be fun and interesting, but it turned out on Sundays, the place was essentially a ghost town. The only place open was the gas station and even that only had one employee working who lived upstairs.

"Do you want to drive to the next town? Maybe it will be better. I had forgotten what day it was since I haven't been working," Embry said as we got back in the jeep.

"No, it's not a huge deal. Maybe we can order

movies online and play games back at your place," I said, trying not to be disappointed.

"That sounds like a fantastic idea. I'll sneak over to the pack house and grab some snacks, too. We're running low at my place." She grinned as she drove, and I did my best to be happy about the change of plans, but without the distraction of something new, I couldn't get my mind off the other stuff.

Roman had left his pack because of me. I'd hurt him, and I hated that. Plus, I wondered how long I would have to deal with the effects of our bond and how they were affecting Roman as well. Understandably, I doubted I would get that answer.

Tomorrow, I'd have to ask Serene about some more books from the library. I knew Roman had said I was welcome to them, but it didn't feel right anymore. I wouldn't be trying to keep my distance from the rest of the shifters now that they didn't hate me, but I would still be avoiding Roman—respecting his want for a clean break.

I also didn't know what to say to him. As the hours passed since I'd last seen him, guilt grew within me. I hadn't expected the heavy emotions and the worse they got, the more I wondered if I'd made the right choice. If maybe I should have thrown caution to the wind and hoped for the best.

Except that wasn't how I was raised and... well, I didn't really have any other reason except I was scared shitless of the unknown.

We arrived back at the pack and went straight to

Embry's. I tried to tell myself not to look for signs of Roman's arrival, but it was impossible not to.

"Do you want to go pick out a couple of movie choices while I get food?" Embry asked as my stomach growled.

"Hurry with the food," was my only reply as I headed inside.

The house was quiet, and my thoughts were loud. Not a good combination. I grabbed my phone and turned on some music while I searched for something to watch.

I was having a hard time deciding between one so cheesy we could make fun of it or something with more action so that I didn't have to worry about too much romance.

I added several to the watch list and figured Embry could narrow it down when she got back. Glancing at my phone, I realized it had already been nearly thirty minutes that she'd been gone. My stomach started to twist in knots as my energy swirled.

Something was wrong.

I tried to call her cell phone, but it went straight to voicemail. Peeking out the window, I didn't see anything out of the ordinary, but my heart was still beating like crazy.

I didn't have anyone else's phone number, and I couldn't do the mind speak stuff, so I either had to stay put or go check things out.

Maybe everything was fine. Maybe someone convinced Embry to stop by the barbecue, but wouldn't she have come back for me if she was staying? Or maybe she got tied up with accounting stuff. She'd put off work for several days just for me. Yeah, that was probably it. Someone needed her for something, and she couldn't get away once they found her.

I paced the living room for another five minutes before I'd had enough. "Screw this," I said as I headed out the door.

My energy was acting erratic, but still sluggish compared to the day before. I needed to remember to breathe. Embry was a wolf shifter. She was strong and smart. Nothing had happened to her. I was being ridiculous.

My steps quickened as I got closer to the pack house. A group of people were headed in the same direction, and I got even more nervous to the point where I was afraid a panic attack was near.

Shifters had good hearing. They'd know my heart was racing. I had to calm the hell down. There was nothing wrong if people were just walking around.

I recognized two of them from my first day in the pack. I waved, trying to act casual. "Hey, Ginger," I said to the girl, but I couldn't remember the guy's name.

"Hi, Cait. Are you joining the pack for lunch? We're having a special celebration today," she said with zero hostility in her voice.

"Oh, um, well, I was actually looking for Embry. Have you seen her?" I asked.

One of the others stepped forward. "She went with Serene. Not sure where they were going."

Weird. I would have thought Embry would bring me along if Serene was involved in whatever they were doing.

"Well, that explains why she didn't come back then. I'll just go wait for her. You guys enjoy the celebrations," I said, not feeling comfortable going to something like that without Embry.

"Are you sure you don't want to join us?" Ginger pressed.

"Who isn't joining us?" Roman's voice sounded from the opening door.

My hands began to shake and my heart ached from being so close to him, but knowing I would cause him nothing other than pain.

"Cait. She said she's going to wait for Embry," the other girl said.

Roman nodded. "Can you all help Rose get the food taken out back please?"

Shit. He wanted to talk. I doubted that would be good for either of us. Especially not with all the guilt I was battling. I needed to be sure of what I wanted before we had any other serious conversions. I tried to back away slowly, but his eyes met mine and I froze, helpless to do anything other than stare at the silver flecks in his eyes.

Once the others were inside with the door shut, Roman stepped closer to me. "How are you doing?" he asked.

"Great. I've been making lots of progress in training. I heard you went on a trip," I said.

He ran a hand through his long strands. "Yeah, something like that. I'm glad you're doing well. Are you sure you don't want to join us? The pack is all eating together out back. There are blankets and tables and the pups are running around. It's the monthly birthday celebrations. Nobody will bother you."

It actually sounded like a lot of fun, but I couldn't. Not yet. "Maybe next time. I'm really tired. I'm just going to go rest at the cabin."

He nodded. "Get some rest, then. I'll let Embry know I saw you if I see her."

Roman went to the door. He paused when his fingers wrapped around the handle. I sucked in a breath, wondering if he'd look back. Seconds ticked by as the air stilled, but he didn't turn around.

Damn it. I needed to get out of there.

I started walking back to the cabin, ignoring the sounds of kids yelling and adults laughing from behind the pack house.

Seemed like I'd be watching a movie by myself for the afternoon. Hopefully, I could scrounge up some food within Embry's kitchen.

As I stepped onto the path, a shadow moved in front of me. I shoved my hands out on instinct, and Serene fell to the ground.

"Oh, I'm so sorry," I said as I scrambled to help her up.

She hissed at me, then forced a smile. "It's okay, Cait. I was coming to get you anyway."

My mark was pulsing. "I thought you were with Embry."

"She's at the pack house now. I wanted to check with her before I spoke with you. Come on." Serene grabbed on to me, but I jerked my hand back.

"What did you find?" I asked, hesitant to go with her. She was acting stranger than usual.

"An answer to all of your problems," she said with glee.

I stared back at her, confused. "I don't understand."

"I found a way to get rid of your magic."

29

CAIT

Serene led me deep into the trees. The further we got from the main area of the pack, the more my internal warning system screamed at me. Serene was weird every day, but her silence and rush to get away from the pack were suspicious.

"Why aren't we going to your house?" I asked when we seemed to be headed in the opposite direction.

"Because things like this require space," she answered without slowing down.

I reached for her. "Wait a minute. What is it that you're going to do to me?"

She sneered at my hand wrapped around her forearm, and something foreign filtered through me, but the harshness of her tone distracted me.

"First, don't touch me. Second, I'm going to give you what you want. Or have you changed your mind?" she sneered.

I jerked away from her. "I don't know. You're not

telling me anything. Beatrix already warned us I could die and I'm not ready to risk my life. Now, tell me what we're doing out here."

Serene's eyes narrowed, darker than normal. "Why do you have to ask so many questions? You're making me think you're ungrateful. Is that what you are, Cait? Just another ungrateful human?"

Shock tore through me. "What's wrong with you?"

She straightened, calming some after a deep breath. "Sorry. It's been a long day. It would be really helpful if you'd stop asking questions. I already talked to Beatrix. That's where I was today. I know what I'm doing."

Yeah, that didn't work for me.

"Just tell me why we're out here alone," I said.

Serene stepped toward me again, getting in my face. "Because we're keeping everyone else safe. You wouldn't want to have your energy backfire and hurt someone who was too close, right?"

"What do you mean?" If I was concerned before, I was freaking the hell out now, but my thoughts began to slow causing the seriousness of my voice lessened.

Power swirled inside me, trying to get free, but it was weaker, more so than earlier in the day, and seemed to keep depleting the further we got from the pack.

"I mean that if you want the bond to be broken, then we have to get the magic out of you that created it. I know how to do that now. So, let's get moving before the celebrations are over and there are wolves running through the forest. Like I said, you wouldn't want anyone to get hurt, right?"

"You can break the bond and remove the supernatural stuff from me?" I asked for clarification. For some reason her words were not making sense to my suddenly foggy brain.

"Jesus, girl. You're not near as strong as I thought you were." Serene jerked on my arm, and I barely stayed on my feet as I stumbled after her.

I didn't know much about this world, but this wasn't right. Serene wasn't thinking clearly. Something had happened, and I wanted to know what.

Yet, I wasn't in any position to stop Serene or run away from her. I wanted to call for Embry and have her confirm this was normal, but I also didn't want to further agitate Serene.

Finally, we stopped and she turned, a smirk on her face. "Alright, Cait. Let's see what you've got going on inside that weak body."

I held my hand up. "Wait a minute. I'm not sure I want to do this and I have more questions. Why didn't Embry come with you?"

"She really wanted to be here, but like I said, people could get hurt. It was safer for her to stay back at the house. Unlike *some,* she didn't ask many questions. But don't worry, this will only bring the two of you closer. Aren't you tired of her being your constant babysitter? I know she is."

I opened my mouth to reply, but I didn't know what to say and my thoughts were getting jumbled.

The best friend I thought I knew would have told me if I was a bother to her, but maybe the Embry in person and the one I video-chatted with weren't entirely the same. I hadn't known the real her until I arrived in Texas.

"Will I remember any of this when the magic is gone?" I asked once I decided to move past Embry not being present.

"Oh, of course. Don't you worry," Serene said, then hurried over to a tree while I was left standing alone.

I placed my hands over my face as I tried to get my thoughts under control. What was wrong with me? I shouldn't be out here. I needed to get back to the pack house. Alarm bells were going off and a fog was being lifted from my mind as I fought to find some normalcy.

Serene came back with a dagger in her hands. Yeah, I definitely wasn't doing this.

"Oh, calm down. I'm not going to stab you. This is actually for me," Serene said.

"I don't want this. I'm going back to the pack house," I said forcefully.

Serene snarled at me. "You are doing this. I didn't put up with everything I have for this not to happen today. Now, stay still."

Serene gripped my wrist and pulled me close. I tried wiggling away, but another current of something unfamiliar ran through me.

"What are you doing to me?" I asked.

"If you don't want to get hurt, I need you to stay really still. No matter how uncomfortable this is. Do you understand?" Serene asked, ignoring my question and for some ridiculous reason I agreed with her.

"Good. Now, keep quiet." Serene's hands grabbed both sides of my face, and heat scorched my skin. Not the same kind from my energy, but the type that actually felt like it was burning me from the outside in.

My jaw tensed as my muscles itched to punch Serene in her wrinkled face. Except, when I focused on her, the wrinkles were smoothing away, and her eyes were all black.

"Serene?" I asked.

"Shut it, human." The voice no longer belonged to Serene, and I realized too late why she'd seemed so different.

This wasn't Serene.

I had no idea who this woman was, but the more magic she pressed into me, the more her image flickered before my eyes until it changed completely. Gone were the grey hair and wrinkles. In their place was long blonde hair and smooth alabaster skin.

"Who are you?" I demanded, but still felt so weak from whatever the woman had done to me.

"Someone who you're going to make very powerful," she replied, and my previous conversation with Beatrix came to mind. Whoever this was had to be a witch wanting to take my energy.

She didn't seem to be in control of her magic, though, which told me I wasn't going to make her powerful—I was going to kill the both of us. Beatrix had been very clear that taking whatever was inside me wasn't an easy task and needed proper preparation, something I was certain didn't include dragging me through a forest and forcing the energy out of me.

I wrapped my fingers around her hands, trying to pry her off of me, but no amount of force I could muster made a difference.

Not-Serene laughed in my face. "Poor pitiful human. Did you not think I'd be ready for this? You've been weakening all day in preparation for this moment. Nothing is going to stop me from finishing my task. Now, for the last time, be still while I take what's mine, or I will kill you, regardless of what my boss wants."

Realizing I could be wrong and maybe being prepared wasn't as complicated as Beatrix had made it sound, I had to try harder to get away. I wouldn't just roll over and die. If I couldn't overpower her, I could at least be as loud as possible, in hopes someone would hear me and arrive before it was too late.

"They'll kill you," I said right before I sucked in a deep breath and screamed from the bottom of my lungs.

The psycho couldn't cover my mouth without releasing the hold she had on my head. With wolf hearing, someone had to pick up my screams. At least, I hoped like hell they did.

"Scream one more time and I'll snap your neck," Not-Serene snapped at me.

"You're not going to survive this. My energy will kill the both of us before it allows you to take it," I threatened back though my words felt hollow. So much for all of my training coming in handy when I needed it most.

She grinned. "You have no idea what you're talking about. I just need to take my payment and then get you to the man who hired me. Now, quit fighting me and give up the energy you were so eager to get rid of before."

Son of a bitch. This wasn't good.

I was better off dead, from the sounds of it, so I decided to chance another scream. If she needed to get me to someone else, I might have a shot at getting one of the wolves' attention.

Just as I opened my mouth, I heard a howl break through the quiet forest.

"Seems I'm going to have to change my plans. Be a good girl and don't move," she said as she tossed me to the ground.

I had zero intention of staying put, but I couldn't move. Whatever magic the witch had touched me with was causing my muscles to seize, and power itched along my skin. My view at least allowed me to see what was happening around me.

The woman had her back turned toward me and was opening some kind of rift in the air. Within a few seconds, the hole was big enough to walk through and black on the other side.

She bent down to pick me up by the hair. I yelped from the pain, and growls sounded around us as she backed up to the opening. "Sorry, dogs. It's time for us to go," the woman jeered.

Roman's wolf lunged for us, and my heart sank as tears pricked in my eyes.

I'd never see him again. I'd never see Embry, either. I'd made the wrong choice, and this was my consequence.

"I'm sorry," I whispered as Roman reached where I'd been just a fraction of a second too late.

The rift swallowed us up, and my last thoughts were nothing optimistic as consciousness faded away.

I'd made a mistake. One I could never take back.

30

ROMAN

Cait was gone.

Someone had taken her right out from under me, and I was going to hunt down everyone involved. Even if it was the last thing that I did, I vowed to chase them to the ends of the earth and kill them all.

I didn't care that she'd rejected me. Cait was mine to protect. *My mate.*

She's ours, my wolf growled.

An all-consuming fury fueled us as we let out an ear-piercing howl, signaling the pack that a fight had arrived at our doorstep and we wouldn't back down.

My paws pounded on the dirt as I broke into a run and followed the scent of the witch I planned to rip to shreds.

I had to get to Cait. I wouldn't let the haunted look in her eyes as I failed to save her be the last image I had of my mate.

I would get her back no matter the cost.

///

Want to stay up to date on all things Luna Marked? Join my reader group HERE and preorder Wolf Taken HERE. Releasing July 15th, 2021!

STAY IN TOUCH

Find Heather on Facebook:
Reader Group:
Heather Renee's Book Warriors

Author Page:
Heather Renee Author

Or by signing up for her newsletter:
http://smarturl.it/HeatherReneeNL

ALSO BY HEATHER RENEE

Luna Marked

A wolf shifter series (dual POV) featuring a strong-willed leading lady and a patient, yet fierce alpha male.

Broken Court

A complete Urban Fantasy series featuring an unconventional and anti-heroine leading lady, a broody love interest, and a fae kingdom with a vile king.

Royal Fae Guardians

A complete Urban Fantasy series featuring fae, magic users, a sweet romance, along with snark and humor.

Shadow Veil Academy

A complete Urban Fantasy Academy series featuring shifters, elves, witches, and more.

Elite Supernatural Trackers

A complete Urban Fantasy series featuring witches, demons, a smart-mouthed female lead, alpha males, and a snarky fairy sidekick.

Raven Point Pack Series

A complete Paranormal Romance series featuring wolves, witches, vengeance, and fated mates.

Blood of the Sea Series

A complete Paranormal Romance series featuring vampires, open seas adventures, and the occasional pirate.

Standalone

Marked Paradox - A complete Fantasy fae story about a realm divided and one fae to bring them back together.

ABOUT THE AUTHOR

Heather Renee is a *USA Today* bestselling author who lives in Oregon. She writes urban fantasy and paranormal romance novels with a mixture of adventure, humor, and sass. Her love of reading eventually led to her passion for writing and giving the gift of escapism.

When Heather's not writing, she is spending time with her loving husband and beautiful daughter, going on their own adventures. For more ways to connect with her, visit www.HeatherReneeAuthor.com.

www.ingramcontent.com/pod-product-compliance
Lightning Source LLC
Chambersburg PA
CBHW070547310726
48982CB00011B/1496/J

* 9 7 8 1 7 3 5 4 7 4 6 3 2 *